HIGH PRAISE FOR KATIE MAXWELL AND
THE YEAR MY LIFE WENT DOWN THE LOO!

"*The Year My Life Wen*
out-loud funny, full o
realistic teenage angst
the book is impossible

"Gripping, smart-alecky, shocking . . . and at the same time tender. A brilliant debut by Katie Maxwell in the Young Adult forum!"

—*KLIATT*

"Fans of *The Princess Diaries* and other well written teen books will cheer this new entry to the scene."

—*Huntress Reviews*

"Girls of all ages will find themselves laughing out loud at Emily's crazy antics and experi
themselves relating to many of
go through. A great start to a gr

—Erica Soro

"This debut book for Dorchester
a word, refreshing. It's so true t
average teenage girl's issues in
bland subjects covered in many
will laugh, sigh and squeal aloud
Emily's journey."

—*Rom*

WHY MY E-MAILS FROM SCOTLAND ARE BETTER THAN MY E-MAILS FROM ENGLAND

1. Kilts, kilts, kilts! Or rather guys in kilts, guys in kilts, guys in kilts! Hunky hotties in plaid—life just doesn't get too much better!

2. I'm completely unbiased and majorly factual, so you get the real poop on what it's like to slog around in the y, cold, nasty mud with stinky, mean, murderous sheep that hate American teens.

3. I tell you everything, and I mean EVERYTHING about my wild, passionate love affair with Ruaraidh, the eleven-fingered Scottish hottie.

4. I send you the very latest in über-cool slang, stuff like "meh" and "ickle."

5. You get to hear about Holly and her wild, passionate love affair with Ruaraidh, the eleven-fingered Scottish, hot . . . um . . . yeah, both of us. Don't worry, I'll explain it.

6. My direct, unblinking, and TOTALLY TRUE warning against the Horror of Scotland, AKA haggis, which should be worth the price of your Internet connection in itself.

7. Did I mention Ruaraidh? And his eleven fingers? And our snogging contest? Mmmrowr!

THeY weaR **WHAt** uNDeR THeiR KiLts?

Katie Maxwell

SMOOCH NEW YORK CITY

SMOOCH ®

January 2004

Published by

Dorchester Publishing Co., Inc.
200 Madison Avenue
New York, NY 10016

Printed in the United States of America.

Visit us on the web at www.smoochya.com.

This book is dedicated to my adopted grandma, Honey—known to most everyone as Carol Krueger—for all her support and good wishes, and also to Honey's real granddaughter, my darling agent Michelle Grajkowski. You ladies rock! Hugs and kisses to both of you.

THeY weαr **WHAt** uNDer THeir kiLtſ?

Subject: Plaid, plaid, everywhere!
From: Mrs.Legolas@kiltnet.com
To: Dru@seattlegrrl.com
Date: 2 January 2004 8:19pm

Hoots, mon, it's a bracht bricht moonlit nicht!

Yes, yes, we're here in Scotland (note the "while I'm in Scotland" e-mail addy, please), and already things are looking up. First off, there's Alec (I refuse to call him "Uncle Alec" because I'm almost seventeen, *not* a child). Is it illegal for a man to marry his wife's niece? If it's not, hoo, baby, watch out, Emily's in town! I don't care if he is almost as ancient as my father; he's just so scrummy! He's got this really sexy thick accent, the kind that rolls all over you and makes you feel all warm and squidgy inside. Yeah, sure, it's a bit hard to understand him unless you're really concentrating, but no man is perfect, right? Anyhoo, I'd be all Emily the Seductress with him despite his great age, but Aunt Tim gave me one of those squinty-eyed glares that screamed,

"Hands off, younger and much more attractive female! This man is mine!"

I think she's just jealous of my stunning use of cosmetics.

So there we were, the fam (minus Bess; she's off with her BF Monk—I still don't see why she gets to go off on her own just because she's nineteen) and me and Holly—oh, I meant to tell you, Holly finally got the OK to do her work experience here too, which is utterly coolio, because although Alec is a really hottalicious older man, and Aunt Tim is pretty cool for an aunt despite the squinty-eyed glares, they're both elderly with a capital EL. Holly is fun, even though she is a year younger than me, and let me tell you, I'm going to need major copious amounts of fun to survive a whole month out in the middle of the Highlands on this muddy sheep farm. Although it *is* cool that the schools in England have us doing a month of working on a real job. I guess that's one of the bennies about Brother having dragged us to England to live for the year while he does the scholar exchange thing—I get to do work experience, which is going to look so good on my transcripts, don't you think?

I know, I know, you said all along it was a mistake to spend my whole month of work experience on a farm in Scotland, but the only other job I could find was at the library, and you might just as well give up all hope of having *any* sort of cool if you're stuck in the slaves' quarters at a library. Old people work there! If nothing else, the hottie quotient is very low in a library, whereas at least in Scotland there are guys in kilts. I didn't watch all those years of *Highlander* to come here and *not* see guys in kilts!

Where was I? Oh, yeah, so we were all standing around outside Alec's and Aunt Tim's house, bundled up in our coats and scarves and gloves because Scotland is evidently in outer Siberia, looking at mud, mud, a couple of dogs, and, surprise of all surprises, more mud, when all of a sudden, Brother goes completely mental. Not that that's saying much about a man who insists everyone calls him Brother (even Holly calls him Brother now!), but you know just how mental my father can go when he wants to.

"Timandra, I expect that you and Alec will both keep an eye on Emily and Holly while they're here," he said, waggling his unibrow at Aunt Tim and Alec. "And just in case the phrase 'Keep an eye on them' is too vague, let me elaborate."

I groaned and tried to look like Brother hadn't had parent sex with Mom sixteen and three-quarter years ago. No, wait, that's when I was born; that would mean . . . um . . . sixteen years and nine months, plus nine months of Mom being pregnant with me . . . let's see, that would be seventeen years exactly if I borrowed three months from Mom being pregnant, which leaves six left over, except she said I was a bit late in coming, so you have to add on a couple of extra weeks . . . oh, never mind, let's just call it seventeen and a half years ago, 'kay? Back to what I was saying—I tried to look like Brother wasn't really my father. Because, I knew, you see, just what he was going to say.

It had to do with boys. It always has to do with boys; everything Brother talks to me about these days has to do with boys. You should have seen him before Christmas, when I told him I needed some more money to buy Christmas presents.

"For whom?" he asked, all suspicious and nosy. Have I told you he's started to pick up an English accent? Four months in the country and he's saying things like "brolly" for umbrella, and "ta" instead of thanks.

To be honest, I like the *ta* thing, but I'll die before I admit that to him.

Where was I again? Oh, yeah. Before Christmas.

"Fang and Devon," I answered his question (truthfully, because I know Brother likes Fang the best of all my guy friends, although he's not too hot on Devon ever since Devon's party, when I barfed all over him because I was drunk).

"You're going to what?" Brother asked, and cocked the unibrow at me in the way he thinks is so intimidating, but really just makes me want to laugh. "You're buying presents for your boy-friends?"

"Bro*ther*!" I said, giving him a Look. Honestly, the things I have to suffer, having a medieval scholar for a father. He is just *so* ancient times! It's all "duty and honor" this, and "no inappropriate touching" that. Are you sure you don't want to trade dads? I'd be happy to put up with your dad's new trophy wife if you want to take Brother. "Devon and Fang aren't my boyfriends, they're just my friends. And I want to buy them Christmas presents not just because they're my very best guy friends, but also because they were so nice about telling Aidan off when he turned out to be the BF from hell."

The Elderly One muttered something about me trying to drive him into an early grave, which is just ridiculous because we both know he's about a hundred years old now, so there's nothing *early* about it. But that was a couple of weeks ago; earlier today I just knew that he was going to embarrass the pants off of me by saying that Alec and Aunt Tim were supposed to protect our honor and guard our chastity with their lives.

". . . and we all know how boy-crazy girls are these days,

so Chris and I expect you to do everything humanly possible to protect their good names and honor against besmirchment, not to mention guarding their chastity like it was a gold-plated . . . er . . . ewe."

"Come along, Brother; the girls will be just fine," Mom said, tugging him toward the car.

"Not that I expect miracles, mind you." Brother dug in his heels and gave Alec that father look (you know, the one that fathers exchange with each other—the one that's almost an eye roll). Alec just looked puzzled, in a hottie-older-man sort of way—he does puzzled much better than Brother. "Do everything you can to keep them chaste, but don't put your life at risk."

"Thanks for the ride to Scotland. I'll e-mail you later," I said loudly. "Time to leave now! Buh-bye!"

"Eh . . ." Alec said, eyeing Holly and me, his view of our extreme coolness obviously being tainted by my father's slander.

"They can spot a boy at distances beyond the range of normal human eyesight, you know," Brother added. Alec looked startled.

"Dear, we really should be starting back. I'm sure Emily and Holly will behave like adults," Mom said, trying to haul Brother over to the car.

Brother's hair ruffled in the wind and formed into his traditional horn of hair that made him look part rhinoceros, part man (with an emphasis on the rhino). "Is that supposed to make me feel better? Good God, Chris, you've armed the girl with condoms and contraceptives and informative pamphlets, and God only knows what else. It's not like the Middle Ages, I can tell you that! Back then, fathers knew what their daughters were up to. They locked the little darlings into towers until the day of their wedding. There's much we can learn from our medieval ancestors. Chastity belts for one."

Aunt Tim snickered, then tried to cover it up by pretending to cough.

"Ohmigod, Brother!" I yelled, and socked him on the arm. "Just embarrass me to death, why don't you?"

"Embarrass you? Nothing embarrasses you!" He turned back to Alec. "You should see the avaricious light that comes to their eyes when they spot a boy. It's positively frightening. The last four months with Emily have taken off at least ten years of my life."

He's going senile, of course. That's the only thing that explains why he talks that way. "You'd better stop somewhere and get a hot-water bottle for Brother," I told Mom. "I think his brain has frozen up."

"Why, just today I was almost trampled to death when we stopped at a mall."

"It wasn't a proper mall; it was a shopping center," I thought it only right to point out. "There was no movie theater, no piercing place, and no pizza! It's not technically a mall if there's no pizza."

"Never cross a teenage girl's line of sight when she has a boy in the crosshairs," he warned Alec. "You're taking your life in your hands if you do."

Aunt Tim snickered again, this time not even trying to make it sound like a cough. I let Brother glare at her because I was too busy trying to set things straight. "Oh, for Pete's sake, all we did was go around you so that really cute guy wearing the kilt wouldn't know you were with us."

"They shoved me to the ground, both of them. If I hadn't been quick, they would have run right over the top of me to get to some knobby-kneed kid in a kilt standing outside a music store."

"Brother lives in his own little fantasy world. We humor him as much as possible," I told Aunt Tim. I figured that, as his sister, she should be the first one to know the truth about him.

"Ah! There, do you see? That's the look, the one Holly is wearing. That's your warning sign, Alec. If you see either of them wearing that look, run for cover, lest you be trampled to death in their lust to get their clutches on some unwary male."

I looked over at Holly to see what on earth Brother was making such a fuss about. Holly stood stiff as a rock, her eyes huge, her mouth hanging open as she stared down toward the big barn across the yard. I turned to look, and just about fell on my butt in surprise.

A hunk, a hottie, a god in jeans and a black leather jacket walked out of the barn toward us. He was the most drool-worthy, hottalicious, utterly coolio boy I've ever in my whole entire life seen, and that includes seeing Orlando Bloom live and in person at the Hard Rock Café in London (I know you're not into *The Lord of the Rings* or Legolas, but I'm sorry, Orlando as the Leg Man is just too nummy for words). This guy was tall, had long red hair (red!) that brushed his shoulders, and the most amazing walk!

I stared at him, and I have to admit, I almost drooled. Really, I almost drooled; I could feel the slobber gathering on my tongue. I had to swallow a couple of times; it was that bad. I grabbed Holly's arm as the vision of hunkitude walked toward us, and she grabbed mine. He was so fabu, we had to prop each other up to keep from falling over into a major faint. No, wait, fabu isn't good enough—he was mondo coolio *über*-fabu!

"Who . . . who . . . who . . ." I couldn't get the words out because my tongue was broken. It felt all swollen and huge, like it was glued to the top of my mouth.

"Who is that?" Mom asked, nodding toward the red-headed god as she gave me one of her pitying looks. I tried to smile at her in appreciation, but I think my lips were broken too, because they didn't smile properly; they just kind of hung there, flapping in the wind.

Everyone turned to look at the boy, who stopped to pat one of the black-and-white sheepdogs.

"Ah. That'll be Rwawruahwr."

I know, I know, but I swear to you that's what it sounded like Alec said. It started with an R and kind of turned into a gargle, but I didn't care. This guy could be named Booger and my heart would still be his.

"Who?" Brother asked, narrowing his eyes.

"Rwawruahwr," Alec said again. "He's helping me out for a few months while Mark is in New Zealand."

Mark is Alec's shepherd. He's kinda nice, but really, really old—almost fifty.

"Rrrrwowry?" Brother asked, his unibrow all scrunched up.

"Mmmrrrowr," I purred, then sucked in my cheeks so I'd look like I had real cheekbones, not the kind that are put on through the skillful use of makeup.

"His name is Rory," Aunt Tim said. "Only it's pronounced the Gaelic way, with a little extra fillip at the beginning, and you roll the Rs. It's spelled R-U-A-R-A-I-D-H."

"Surely you jest," Brother said, flaring his nostrils, which, I have to tell you, is not a pretty sight, since he's evidently growing the Redwood Forest of nose hairs in there. I made a mental note to remind Mom she needs to break out the pruning shears, then turned my attention back to where it was meant to be. "How old is he? He looks like he's about eighteen or nineteen."

"Eighteen," Alec said.

Holly's hand tightened on my arm as the gorgeous hunk of flesh straightened up and smiled at us. Eighteen! He was eighteen! How *very* fortunate that I like older men!

"Um. Does he . . . uh . . . have a girlfriend?" I asked, figuring it was worth risking the embarrassment of asking the question in order to find out.

"Oh, God, eighteen and male." Brother groaned, and put his hands over his face. Mom patted his arm and made soft little murmuring noises in his ear.

Beside me, Holly squeaked. She does that when she's excited. I'm trying to break her of the habit, but you know how it is—once a squeaker, always a squeaker.

"I'm of a mind he doesn't," Alec said, giving me a thoughtful look. "But you might be wantin' to ask the lad himself that, Emily."

"No, no, no. It's doomed, the whole visit is doomed," Brother said, still moaning into his hands.

No girlfriend! Bwahahahahah! He's mine, all mine! Well, he would be as soon as one formality was taken care of. . . .

"Dibs the hottie," I said at exactly the same time that Holly whispered, "Bagsies, he's mine!"

Bagsies, unfortunately, are the same as dibs. Rats.

"I called dibs first," I whispered back, my words a bit slurred because it's hard to talk with your cheeks sucked in.

"No, you didn't, I bagsied him before you finished your sentence."

"Hullo," Ruaraidh said as he came up to where we were all standing next to the car. "You must be Timandra's family. I'm Ruaraidh Andrews."

He held out his hand for Brother to shake. I managed to get my lips working again, and tried to look very coolio and casual and all that while still maintaining my cheekbones. Brother stared at Ruaraidh's hand like it was made up of toads or something.

"He's got six fingers," Brother said hoarsely. I blinked at him a couple of times, then looked down at Ruaraidh's hand. He was right, Ruaraidh, the Scottish god of love, had six fingers on his right hand. *Six fingers! Ohmigod!*

"Dear God, he's eighteen, male, and has six fingers on one hand," Brother said, turning to Mom. "I hope you're happy, Chris; I just hope you're happy! Because *you* said she would be fine up here for a month, we're going to have grandchildren with twelve fingers."

"Grandchildren?" Ruaraidh's eyes opened up really wide as he turned to look at me. I tried to smile at him. I couldn't. I was too mortified.

"Um . . . I'm adopted. He's not my real father. In fact, I don't even know him. He was hitchhiking by the side of the road when we drove up here. My mom thought it would be fun to pretend he was my father. Ha ha ha," I said, praying he would think I was telling the truth.

Holly said something that sounded like, "Gark!" I knew just how she felt.

Two dark red eyebrows swooped upward over beautiful dark greenish-grayish eyes. He obviously didn't believe me.

Brother took a deep breath and started into another lecture about us not committing any "carnal acts" (his words,

10

not mine). Fortunately, Mom got him into the car before he could do too much more damage, but all things considered, it was too late.

So that's it, Dru. One day in Scotland and my life is officially over. The most delicious boy on the entire planet not only has six fingers on one hand, but he also thinks my father is one green maraschino cherry short of a fruitcake, and I'm some sort of superslut who wants to have his children even though I'm not even seventeen yet.

This is going to be a *very* long month.

Hugs and kisses,
~Em

Subject: re: Six fingers? SIX??? Are you sure?
From: Mrs.Legolas@kiltnet.com
To: Dru@seattlegrrl.com
Date: 3 January 2004 7:51am

Dru wrote:
> I can't believe you go to Scotland and the very first thing
> you do is see a guy in a kilt (*swoon*) and a hottalicious
> Scottish love god (*thud*). Do you know the odds of that
> happening are like a gazillion to one? TELL ME MORE
> ABOUT RURAUGHIDH!!!

It's Ruaraidgh. No, wait, Ruaraight. Um. Ruariadh? Yeah, I think that's it. He's . . . Oh, Dru, he's just soooooooooqoo slobbericious. I've drooled at least five gallons of drool during the last twelve hours.

OK, let me get to the nitty-gritty on him:

- Name: starts with an R. Not sure on the rest of the letters.
- Height: about five-foot-ten, which is just perfect, don't you think? Not too tall, but not short, either. Perfect kissing height. Yay!
- Weight: dunno, but he's not too skinny. Could be buff; hard to tell with the sweaters and jeans he wears.
- Eyes: dreamy. Well, OK, technically they're kind of a grayish-greenish hazel, but he's got dark red eyelashes and it makes his eyes look really nummy.
- Total finger count: eleven. I'm not quite sure what's up with that; I didn't have a chance to ask him about it because Holly hogged the conversation last night at dinner and I couldn't just come right out and say, "Please pass the potatoes, and oh, what's with that extra finger," now, could I?

The extra one is on his right hand, BTW, at the end. Kind of like an extra pinkie. And no, before you ask, it doesn't look gross or mangled or alien or anything. He just has an extra finger. I have to admit it's kind of . . . odd. Strange. OK, it's downright weird, but the rest of him is so drool-worthy, I'm willing to put up with a little bit of finger strangeness to get the rest of him.

And speaking of *that,* I had a talk with Holly last night.

"I think we need to talk," I said to her when we went up to bed. We're sharing the spare bedroom, which isn't too bad, although Holly bagsied the mondo-cool daybed before I could, so I have to sleep under a drafty window. We were unpacking our stuff, and I thought it was time we got a few things straight.

"About what?" she asked, watching as I set out my

makeup on the little vanity table. "I thought you weren't going to bring all your makeup?"

I lined up the five fingernail polishes, the three powders (day, evening, and glittery for special occasions), the blushes (only brought four of them), twelve lipsticks, two lip liners, four lip glosses (both flavored sparkly, and flavored non-sparkly for serious events), lip smoother and plumper, the three basic mascaras that you know I don't go anywhere without, only *one* eyeliner, the three-tiered case of forty-eight eye shadows, three cover-ups (buff, cremora, and zit-zapper white), two moisturizers, four body lotions, lemon butter cuticle cream, five bath oils (luscious lemon, gardenia, strawberry, zesty ocean, and passionate mango), three body dusters, two spritzers, avocado face mask, two toners (oily and normal), apricot and orange scrubs, and, of course, the hair stuff (hot rollers, conditioner, clay packs, hair spray, mousse, styling gel, and three shampoos).

"I didn't," I said, looking in my bag for my velvet body rub (I think I left it at home). "I only brought the bare necessities. Why do you ask?"

She looked at the edge of the table, where her stuff was scrunched up (she only brought *one* of everything! For a whole month! Have you ever???). "No reason. What did you want to talk to me about?"

I gave her the moue of *you know exactly what i'm talking about*. "Ruaraiughd. In specific, your bagsy upon him when you know good and well that I have seniority, and thus have first dibs on all the really hot guys."

She snorted and put a bunch of CDs and her CD player on the floor next to the daybed. "Seniority? I don't know what you're talking about."

"Yeah, well, that's because you're the junior member of

this team." I shook out my pink baby-doll nightie (the one with the little red hearts, and hot-pink feathers on the top). "I'm the senior partner of the firm of Emily and Holly; therefore all hotties go to me by default."

"I don't remember agreeing to that," she said as she got into her plaid flannel jammies. Flannel! I would have said something about how unsexy flannel is, but Holly's the sensitive type, and her feelings would get hurt if she found out that she and my grandma were the only people on the face of the entire planet to wear flannel to bed. "I have just as much right as you do to a really scrummy guy. More, because I don't have a boyfriend and you have Fang and Devon and Aid—"

I gave her Aunt Tim's patented squinty-eyed glare, and got into my pink baby-doll. "Aidan is no longer my BF, and you know it."

She blushed a little and played with the fringe on her flannel jammies (fringed flannel—can you possibly get any more uncoolio than that? I think not). "Sorry. I forgot."

I didn't buy that for a second, but she's my friend, so I couldn't tell her what I really thought. "Whatever. The point is, I'm perfect for Riadraidh and you're not, so it makes sense that I should get him."

"Perfect?" she asked, giving me the Eyebrow of Questioning. "Perfect how?"

You know I like Holly; she's my best friend in England (whereas you are my BFF). She's sweet and smart, and has come a long way in the last few months, ever since I decided she needed a serious fashion makeover, but there are limits to friendship, and when someone says "Perfect how?" in a voice that sounds like the person speaking is secretly laughing, well, then, lines have to be drawn.

14

I straightened up and did my best impression of Brother lecturing one of his medieval-history classes (in other words, I looked really dull). "There are many reasons why I am perfect for Rairuagh. First, I am older than you."

"Only by a year," she said, sitting down on the daybed and hugging Julian, the ratty old teddy bear she brought with her.

"Yes, but once I have my birthday in April, he'll only be one year older than me. You won't be sixteen until June. That's a huge difference in years!"

She snorted again.

"Second, I'm perfect for him because we both have red hair."

"Yes, but yours isn't real; it's dyed. And it's not really red; it's kind of orange."

I climbed into bed. "Copper Sunset Splendor isn't orange; it's copper. Ish. And copperish is almost the same as red."

"Still, you're not a redhead naturally."

"So?"

She did a little pouting thing. "So that means you can't count that on your perfect list, because it's artificial, not real."

I sighed. Sometimes you have to make allowances for friends. "Fine, I'll take that one off the perfect list. Happy now?"

"No. I think I should have a chance with Ruaraidh, too."

"Third," I said quickly, "I'm perfect for him because we like the same sorts of things."

"Second," Holly said.

"What?"

"That is your second item, because you removed the red-hair perfection."

I'm starting to think it was a mistake to nag her into coming up here for her month of work experience. "Second! Second, I'm perfect for him because we like the same things."

"What sort of things?"

I blinked at her. I just *knew* she was going to ask that. "Um. Things. You know . . . um . . . sheep and Scotland and sweaters and stuff."

She nibbled on her lower lip for a moment. "You told me that sweaters were dead grotty unless they were angora or mohair, and came from Cruise or Harvey Nichols. Ruaraidh's sweater was knitted. He said his mum knits him sweaters because he spends so much time outdoors."

"I knit," I said. Yes, yes, that wasn't strictly the truth, but I had my fingers crossed, and I fully intend on learning how to knit, so it's almost the truth. Aunt Tim said at dinner how nice Rauraiugh's sweater was, and he said he loves them, so you see that it's vitally important that I learn how to knit. It can't be hard, I mean, it's just twisting a bit a wool around on one of those long shiny knitting things, right?

"You do?"

"Sure. I haven't . . . uh . . . done it in a while, but I knit. In fact, I was thinking of knitting the R-man a sweater."

She got an obstinate look on her face. "So was I; I was thinking about knitting him a sweater, too."

"Oh, really? Er . . . how long have *you* knitted?"

"Since I was seven. I won honorable mention two years in a row at the Girl Guides' Textile Fair."

Crap. Double crap. Just my luck, of all the girls in the Piddlesville area to pick as my best friend, I have to pick the world-champion knitter. "Oh. OK. Guess we'll both be knitting for him, then, huh?"

16

She nodded. "You don't like sheep, either, so that's a fib."

"I don't fib; I never fib. I do, too, like sheep . . . they look really pretty on a hill."

She made a face. "You meant that you like sheep like Ruaraidh likes them, not that you like to eat them. Besides, he's a vegetarian."

"He is?"

She nodded again.

Rats! How could I have missed that? I was watching him like a hawk all during dinner. Oh, well, I'm not known for my *über*-coolness for nothing. I shrugged and said, "Oh, yes, I knew that; I just didn't know *you* knew that."

"You told me you thought Scotland was dreary and cold and smelled funny."

"Boy, you have a mind like an elephant, don't you?"

She sniffed and looked a bit offended. "Well, you did say that."

I climbed into bed with my CD player and headphones. "Yeah, well, I've changed my mind. I like Scotland; it's got a lot of potential, BF-wise. I mean that hottie at the mall in the kilt . . ."

I fanned myself and she grinned, which made me feel better, because I don't like it when Holly is miffed at me.

"He was cute, wasn't he?"

"Sweet," I said, all knowingish. "V. sweet."

She chewed on her lip for a few minutes while I got my CDs set up so I could fall asleep listening to Pink. "Emily, I know you're much cooler than me—"

There wasn't much I could say to that. I mean, *I am*! But Holly is my friend, and you know how I am—I want all my friends to feel just as fabu as they can. "Well, that's true, but you have greatly improved on the coolness scale, so it's really a close call."

She looked surprised and pleased at the same time. "It is? I've improved?"

"Fifteen points at least," I said, setting the CD player to random.

"Fifteen?"

"It would have been twenty, but I had to deduct a few points for the flannel jimjams," I said gently.

She looked down at her jammies. "Oh. Well, anyway, I know I'm not as cool as you are, and I don't have Copper Sunset Splendor hair, just boring old brown hair—"

"Walnut, not brown."

Her mouth hung open a moment. "Walnut?"

"Walnut sounds better than brown. Go on."

She blinked a couple of times, then took a deep breath and spoke really fast. "I know I'm not as cool as you or as pretty or anything like that, but I do think I should have a chance with Ruaraidh because I really like him, and I thought maybe you would agree to let me try for him, too."

I pulled one of the little earphone buds out of my ear. "Are you by any chance suggesting we have a competition?"

She bit her lower lip. "I guess so."

A contest. Hmm. I looked at her sitting on the daybed. In her flannel jammies, with her hair in braids, she looked about twelve. "Goal?"

Her eyes went all round. "What?"

"What's the goal? A date with Ruaraibgh? Snogging him? Doing it?"

"It?"

I raised one eyebrow and gave her a Look. *It.*

"Oh!" She blushed. "I don't . . . I couldn't . . . I haven't . . . and you haven't either . . . Uh . . . how about snogging? First one to snog him wins."

I raised the other eyebrow. "Just snog him?"

She looked worried for a moment, then raised her chin and looked down her nose at me. "No. Proper snogging, with tongues and . . . and . . ."

"Groping?"

"Lots of it," she said, shaking her braids back in a reckless sort of way.

"Hooo," I said, thinking about it. Don't get me wrong, I was a) v. confident that Ruaraidght would prefer the more adult *moi* over Holly, and b) enjoying the thought of snogging him, but you know what can happen when friends go after the same guy—that horrible Guy Destructive Power is unleashed, and no friendship can survive the strain. I didn't want to lose Holly, but at the same time, Ruaraichdhgh really made my toesies curl.

"Rules?" I asked, half hoping she'd drop the idea of us both competing for Ruaraur . . . oh, whatever his name is.

"No saying bad things about each other to him."

"Agreed," I said.

"No pity snogs."

I gave her another Look. "I have never in my life had to play on a guy's sympathy to get a kiss, and I'm not about to start now, when I'm in my prime!"

"You have to wear the clothes you brought with you; no going out to the shops and coming home with Victoria's Secret things."

I sighed. "That won't be a problem. I'm down to my last ten pounds until Brother shells over my next month's allowance."

"No . . . um . . . touching him. *There.*" Her face went bright red as she spoke.

Groppage: been there, done that (well, all right, I haven't, but I could have if I had wanted to), no big deal. "Fine. No touching in the weenus region. Anything else?"

"No, I think that covers everything."

I got out of bed and stood next to hers, holding out my hand. She shook it. "May the best woman win."

"Yes," she said, v. seriously. "Good luck."

I smiled and patted her on the head before climbing back into bed and stuffing the earbuds into my ears. "Same to you. Holly?"

"What?"

"Even if you win, you'll still be my friend."

Her eyes got a bit watery. "Oh, you, too, Emily. You'll be my friend if you win, that is. You'll always be my friend. You're . . ." She looked down and twisted her flannel fringe in her fingers. "You're the best friend I've ever had. I'm so glad you came to England."

I didn't want her to cry or anything, because you know how I am—if anyone cries around me, I cry too, and then my nose fills up and I turn into a giant snot locker. So I just nodded and turned out my light, cranking up my CD player. I tell you, Dru, she looked so sincere, it made me feel bad for thinking of all the things I was going to do to snatch Ruaruaraughugh out from under her nose.

I'm still going to do it, mind you, but now I'll feel bad when I win.

Hugsies and smoochies,
~Em

20

Subject: re: The Competition
From: Mrs.Legolas@kiltnet.com
To: Dru@seattlegrrl.com
Date: 3 January 2004 5:20pm

Dru wrote:
> if you would figure out how to spell his name! I can't
> stand seeing Ruarauightdhauradh anymore!

OK. I wrote it down and stuck it on a posty on Aunt Tim's computer. It's Ruaraidh. Got it.

> And what is it with you and this v. stuff? V? What's that
> supposed to mean?

It's "very," you idget! Only here everyone just says "v" with a period after it, which is just v. tight, don't you think?

Well, I survived my first day here, which is pretty amazing when you consider what I had to do—I had to go out with sheep! Actual wild animals! I could have been *killed*!!!

OK, maybe not killed, but possibly maimed or disemboweled or something like that. And what is with that smell? Sheep stink! Uck!

Let me do this properly, so you fully appreciate the hell that is now my life. There I was this morning, sitting in my pink baby-doll drinking some of my Aunt Tim's coffee (Starbucks "Strong Enough to Trot a Horse on" blend) in an attempt to wake up my brain, and Alec walks in and looks at me and Holly (she was dressed—she's one of those horrible morning people) and says, "Ah, good, you're both up. Just as soon as you've had your breakfast, you can come out to the barn with me, and we'll get started on the mornin' chores."

"Barn?" I asked, adding more cream to my coffee (Aunt Tim likes it strong enough that you can stand a spoon up in it). "Chores?"

"Aye, barn chores. You and Holly. You did come here to earn your work experience, did ya not?"

Oh, yes, it's v. fabu how Alec talks, but when he says stuff like "chores," not even a hunky Scottish accent makes it something you want to investigate further. Clearly Alec was under the impression that I was a new slave that he could order around however he liked. Obviously I needed to set him straight about just what sorts of things I would do for this work-experience business. "Well, as I said last night, my strong suit is in computer skills, so I'd be happy to computerize your sheep records for my work experience."

Holly nodded. "Oh, yes, Mr. McGregor, she's very good at computers. In fact, Emily said on the way up here just how keen she is to do her work experience on the computer rather than with the sheep."

I said that? Yeah, it was the truth, but I don't remember saying it. Still, it was awfully nice of Holly to try to help me.

Alec shook his head. "You did mention the computer, but I'm not needin' my records computerized, and I *am* needin' a few extra hands out on the hills, so that's what I'm askin' you both to be doin'."

"Hills? You mean . . . out in the mud?" I looked from Alec to the window. "It's raining!"

"Aye, that it is. It doesn't change the fact that I'm needin' you both on the hills today."

"I like the rain! I like sheep, too. A few years ago, I spent the summer on my grandparents' farm. I like all animals. I'll be happy to help you out on the hills," Holly said hopefully.

Perhaps I'd made an error when assuming that spending the month here was going to be a piece of cake. "I think I see the problem: you're under the impression that our work experience means *any* sort of work, and we're here to learn *practical* skills. I'm going to be a physicist. Herding sheep around in the mud and rain isn't going to be a skill that will help me in the world of quarks and superconductors. So it doesn't make sense to have me out doing sheepy stuff that has no relationship to physics, or technology in general."

"I want to be a vet," Holly said. I blinked at her. I thought she wanted to be a teacher? "Working with you and . . . uh . . . the sheep will be very beneficial to me."

"I'm sure if you tried hard, Emily, you could find a relationship," Aunt Tim just *had* to say as she set a plate of waffles on the table. "You chose to come here."

Why is it older relatives always like to point out things like that?

"Well, I *assumed* you'd be open to reason about the whole work-experience thing," I said, giving Aunt Tim a glare.

Alec ignored me. That lost him several hottie-older-man points. "This mornin' we'll round up the sheep and start the dosin' for fluke."

Dosing? Fluke? He was speaking pure alien by that point, so I didn't pay any attention to it, instead focusing on what was important—me. "Yes, but I don't want—"

"You'll learn valuable skills here; that I promise you," Alec said, snagging two waffles.

"Dosing sheep sounds like fun," Holly said.

"I'm sorry, but I just don't think fluking a sheep is going to do much to get me into Princeton," I pointed out. Reasonably, I'll have you know, which is saying a lot, since it was morning and everything, and you know how I hate mornings.

"I'd like to learn how to fluke," Holly said.

"Fluke isn't an action, girls; it's a disease of the liver. Alec doses the sheep to keep them from getting sick."

Ew! Sick sheep livers! I hope it's not contagious. "That is my point exactly! How does helping the sheepsies keep their livers clean qualify as a valuable skill?"

"I think knowing about fluke is a very valuable skill for someone who is going to be a vet," Holly said.

"Workin' here will teach you the ability to see a job through to the end, honorin' commitments, followin' orders, workin' together as a team, and fulfillin' an obligation you made," Alec said, cocking an eyebrow at me. Meh! (That's the British equivalent to "gah," BTW). "It's a busy time, dosin' all of the hirsels (note: I asked Aunt Tim later— hirsel means a bunch of sheep. Why can't they just say "bunch of sheep" instead?) is a big job, and we'll need both of you to help."

"I'll do anything you want," Holly said, a wee tad bit desperately, I thought. I gave her a quick look to see what her problem was, but she was too busy watching the door to give me any clue.

"There, you see? Holly will be glad to dose as many sheep as you like." I felt bad about throwing Holly to the sheep, so to speak, but my survival for the next month was at stake. If I didn't want to end up out in the mud giving sheep liver shots, I'd have to make a stand now. "You won't need me if you have her."

She nodded her head rapidly, peering out of the rain-streaked window. "Yes, I'll be happy to help you however you like with the sheep, so Emily can stay here and work on the computer."

Unfortunately, Alec also decided to take a stand. He frowned at me and said, "If you're not wantin' to help out here, Emily, I'm sure we can arrange your trip back to your parents."

I was just going to make it absolutely clear that although I would be as helpful as I could, I drew the line at doing things to sheeps' livers, but then he walked in. Ruaraidh. The Scottish god of everything manly and hot.

Suddenly Holly's desire to work out in the mud was made extremely clear. What a devious mind she has! I can't believe she tried to oust me from spending quality time with Ruaraidh! Meh!

"Morning," Ruaraidh said, smiling at me (and, I have to admit, Holly). His eyes widened a little when he took in my baby-doll nightie with the pink feathers, and of course I had to suck in my cheeks so he would think I had naturally high cheekbones, which meant I couldn't eat, but that was a small sacrifice to pay for true love. "I've milked Mabel, Alec, and fed the dogs. Are we dosing today? I'm ready to go whenever you are."

Alec looked at me. I looked back at him. He did an eyebrow waggle. I turned to smile at Ruaraidh (I'm not entirely sure the sucked-in-cheeks-to-give-me-cheekbones smile was a success—it felt kind of weird, and Ruaraidh's eyes got even wider when I did it).

"Holly and I just love dosing flukes," I de-cheeked long enough to say. "That's all she could talk about on the way up here, and I, of course, love anything to do with sheep and Scotland and sweaters, including knitting them— sweaters, that is, not knitting sheep or flukes; what size sweater do you wear, by the way?—so we're game for a full day of sheep fluking. Alec, pretty please, promise us we'll get to fluke all day!"

Alec's lips twitched, and Aunt Tim walked really quickly into the pantry and started making odd snorting noises (she's old, you know), and Holly gave me a look that on anyone else I would say was pissed. Ruaraidh—who was the only person in the room who really mattered—looked pleased. He smiled at me (just me this time, which I think is worth five points). "Like sheep then, do you?"

"Love them," I said, and gave him a sultry look over my feather-bedecked shoulder. Holly kicked me under the table, but I'm sure it was just because she was mad she didn't have the smarts to show up at the breffie table in a seductive baby-doll.

So, long story short—we went out on the hill and played sheep cowboys. Um . . . I guess that would be sheepboys, wouldn't it? Or sheepgirls, since we're female and all. Sheepgirl Holly and I got all dressed up in our jeans and big rubber boots that Aunt Tim had Mom buy for me, called, for some reason, Wellingtons (or wellies for short). Why would they name rubber boots after some military guy? Did they even have rubber in those days? Honestly, these people can be so strange!

Anyhoodles, off we went in our wellies and coats (Holly called hers an "anorak," but I just refuse to let myself go like that), following Alec and Ruaraidh. Alec was saying something about how the sheep were laid out on the hills and how we were supposed to round them up, but I didn't pay much attention to that because I was watching the dogs.

OK, time-out while I tell you about the dogs. Now, you

know I love dogs, and I still cry whenever I think of Pot Pie dying of doggy cancer, but the dogs here are amazing! They're like superdogs! Alec and Aunt Tim have five dogs, all Border collies (they're black and white, and two of them have long coats, while the other three have short coats), named Rob, Roy, Biorsadh (I had to ask about that spelling, not abso-positively sure on it), Lass, and Brae.

Now, here's what's really cool—Ruaraidh also likes dogs! He's got two Border collies, only his are kind of a rusty red and white, not black and white. His dogs' names are Kaylee and Sandy.

"So what exactly do the dogs do out here?" I asked Ruaraidh as we were walking through seventeen million miles of mud to get to some rocky-looking hill at least five days' march from the house.

"You've never seen sheep dogs?" he asked.

"I have," Holly said quickly, and smiled at him. He smiled back, darn his adorable and utterly snogworthy lips. "You use whistles to make them move the sheep around, right?"

"That's right," Ruaraidh said, smiling some more at her. I gritted my teeth. Holly's knowing about sheep dogs was worth ten points, which meant that so far she was ahead of me in the battle for Ruaraidh. "Each dog has its own whistle that means its name, so when we're out with a number of dogs, we can give a specific dog a command."

"Why don't you just tell them what you want to do?" I asked, fluttering my lashes at him so he smiled at me, too.

Alec laughed and waved a hand toward a small group of sheep that were grazing on the side of the hill. "A whistle can be heard farther than a voice. Brae, lass?"

One of the black-and-white dogs loped over to Alec and looked at him expectantly. He waved his hand toward the sheep. Brae dropped down onto her belly, watching them intently, kind of quivering with excitement.

"Watch her," Ruaraidh said softly, his eyes all sparkly with excitement. I have to admit, I held my breath to see what was going to happen.

"What's she doing?" I whispered back to him.

Holly came over next to me. *Between* Ruaraidh and me, that is. I thought about punching her on the arm, then decided that was too juvenile.

I pinched her instead.

"She's not going to rush them, is she?" Holly asked, rubbing her side where I pinched her.

Ruaraidh smiled at us both (five points each). "No, Alec wouldn't do that. Brae's just getting the flock's attention."

"All she's doing is lying there," I said. "Oh, wait, now she's moving."

"Down!" Alec yelled, and pulled a long silver whistle out of his pocket.

Brae crouched, but skinnied forward on her belly a few steps.

"I'm warnin' you, Brae!" Alec bellowed. She dropped back down to the ground.

Ruaraidh chuckled. "A good sheep dog can control the sheep with just her eyes. Brae's got a bit more to learn yet, but she's a born herder. You can see how much she wants to be herding the sheep over to Alec."

"Wow," I said, and meant it. It was really cool to see Brae lying there intimidating sheep just by staring at them; then suddenly Alec whistled, and Brae went running around the far side of the herd, rounding them up in a clockwise direction.

"Come bye, Kaylee," Ruaraidh said, and one of his dogs went running off to join Brae.

"Why don't the sheep run away from the dogs?" Holly asked.

"They are, in a fashion," Ruaraidh said as we followed the now-moving group of sheep. "You've heard of fight-or-flight?"

We both nodded.

"Well, from a distance, the sheep don't care much about the dog, but when she comes closer, she will stare at the flock. Because she's just staring and not attacking, the sheep decide that it's safer to put some distance between them and the dog, so they move in the opposite direction. The dog then moves to balance the flock's movement, keeping them where she wants them."

"Major coolio!" I said. "I want to do it! Alec, can I order one of your dogs around?"

Oh, poop, I have to go; dinner is on. I'll be back after din-din to tell you about my experience with the wild and highly dangerous sheep of Dulnain Farm.

(Ruaraidh point total so far—Emily: 15, Holly: 15)

Hugs and kisses,
~Em

Subject: Those wild and wooly sheep (wooly, get it? Ha! I kill me)
From: Mrs.Legolas@kiltnet.com
To: Dru@seattlegrrl.com
Date: 3 January 2004 6:34pm

OK, I'm back. Holly volunteered us to do the dishes, so that took time, because evidently they've never heard of dishwashers up here in Scotland. We had to do them *by hand!!!* Thank God I brought lots and lots of moisturizer.

Now, where was I with the sheep experience today? Oh, yeah, the sheep dogs. You know, I can't help but feel that it's majorly unhip to be thrilled by sheep dogs, but Dru, you have to see them! They're totally amazing! I don't care if anyone thinks it's dullsville; those sheep dogs are just downright coolio, and you know I don't award coolio-ness on just anything!

Alec said both Holly and I could each take charge of one of the dogs, which was very tight until I found out that she got Rob (one of the older dogs who knows how to do stuff), while I got Lass.

Don't get me wrong, I like Lass (I like all of the dogs except Biorsadh, who is really old and doesn't like anyone but Alec), but between you and me, she's a few grapes shy of a fruit salad.

Alec ran through the basic commands of sheep dog talk, then sent Holly and me out to round up a few stray sheep.

"Don't we get whistles?" I asked.

" 'Twould take you too long to learn them," Alec said, sending Brae up to the top of the hill. "The dogs'll respond to your commands if you speak to them firmly enough."

I looked at Lass. She smiled at me and wagged her tail.

"You take Lass and fetch those six sheep on the down-slope, Emily. Holly, you and Rob can fetch the four next to the burn. Ruaraidh and I will lift the hirsel from the hill and meet you down there." He pointed to a gate that led into another pasture. *Lift* is sheep-guy talk. I think it means *move*.

"Um. OK." I looked at the tiny piece of paper where I'd written down the commands he told us. " 'Come bye' is clockwise, 'way to me' is counterclockwise, 'down' is stop, 'steady' is slow down, 'walk up' is approach the sheep, and 'look back' is turn around; you left some sheep behind you."

"That's right," Alec said, grinning. Ruaraidh was grinning, too.

"What?" I asked, putting the paper in my pocket and patting Lass on the head.

"*What* what?" Alec asked, still grinning.

"You're smiling like you think we can't handle this."

"It's not as easy as it looks, lass."

Ruaraidh nodded, his formerly adorable smile going all smug and annoying.

I was so cheesed, I didn't even get squidgy over Alec calling me *lass*. "They're sheep, for Pete's sake! It's not like we're trying to move a smart animal that has a mind of its own! I mean, sheep are . . . like sheep! They do what you tell them, right?"

Alec and Ruaraidh exchanged smug "we're men; we know sheep" looks. "Just keep them moving toward the gate, and Ruaraidh and I will help you gather them in once we've moved the rest of the hirsel off the hill."

"We don't need your help," I said, giving Alec my "I am a goddess" down-the-nose look. "It's only like, what, ten sheep? I think we'll manage. How many are you guys doing?"

"About two hundred."

I only *just* caught myself goggling at Alec, which, as you know, is a very unattractive look, and even though I was peeved at Ruaraidh for his smugness over the sheep, I didn't want him to catch me in midgoggle. So instead I just looked bored. "Oh. Two hundred. 'Kay."

Holly looked a bit worried (her natural state) until I nudged her with my elbow. "Huh? Oh. I'm sure I won't have any problem with my sheep."

I gave her the Glare.

"I mean, I'm sure neither of us will have a problem with our sheep," she said quickly.

Boy, you show the girl a Scottish god of sexy thighs, and she goes all grabby on you!

"You be sure to tell me if you need help," Ruaraidh said. Smugly!

Sexy thighs he might have, but gah! I hate guys who act smug! I grabbed Holly and dragged her away toward the handful of sheep that we were supposed to round up. "If he weren't so drop-dead gorgeous, I'd like to tell him a thing or two," I growled.

"Does that mean you are relinquishing—"

"No," I said quickly, stomping through mud and grass and weeds and lots and lots of sheep poop. "Of course not; I'm not stupid. I just don't like anyone assuming he can do something better than me just because he's a guy."

Holly nodded. "Sexual prejudice is always wrong, but he *does* have experience with sheep, and we don't."

"Experience, schmexperience, it's just sheep! What makes him—Ew! I stepped in it! What makes him think that we can't handle a few commands and a couple of stupid sheep? Come on, Lass; those are our sheep. They look pretty dumb; bet it won't take any time to get them rounded up."

Holly and Rob went down to a small stream, where a couple of sheep were huddled around looking moronic.

I stopped about a hundred yards away from the first of my six sheep, and looked at it. It looked back at me. Well, OK, I think it was looking at Lass, who was walking next to me.

"Good girl, you're already heeling!" I said, patting her on her head. She never took her eyes off the sheep. "Right. We have a job to do, and a smug hottie to teach a lesson to. Um . . ."

I reached into my pocket for the piece of paper with my notes, but it was gone. Poop! I looked back toward where we had come from, but didn't see anything white lying on the ground.

"Well, crap on rye, I suppose I could ask Ruaraidh. . . ." That smug smile flashed in my mind, and I decided right then and there that I'd get my sheep to the gate without his help if I had to carry them. "All right. Lass?"

Her ears pricked up, but her eyes stayed on the sheep. I pointed at the sheep. "Come bye!"

She was off like a cheetah, a black-and-white blur as she ran around the sheep at warp speed, running around and around as she gathered the sheep up into a bunch. It wasn't a big bunch because there were only six, all with black noses and dirty gray coats, but still, they were a bunch, which meant that Lass was doing her job, and I'd show Mr. Smarty Hottie Pants what Team Emily could do.

"Yay us!" I cheered Lass. "OK, now way to me, Lass!"

She spun around and started running in the opposite direction, slowly tightening her circle as the sheep clumped together. "Oh, this is too cool! Let's see, what were the other things you can do? Uh . . . Lass, look back!"

She turned and ran away from the sheep, who must have realized that she was off looking for other sheep, because they suddenly scattered, two of them heading right for me.

"Sheep stampede!" I screamed, and ran in the opposite direction of the thundering hooves. "Lass, come back; I mean, come bye, come bye!"

OK, now, here's the thing: it's impossible to run with any sort of speed or grace while wearing wellies in a muddy, sheep-poopy field, especially when part of the field is on a slope, double especially when you have a stampede of sheep thundering behind you.

Here's the other thing: unlike horses, which won't step on you if you fall down, sheep will stomp all over you. They're just mean that way. And stupid. And they smell awful!

"Ew, ew, ew!" I yelled when one of the stampeding herd stepped on my leg as it tried to jump over me. "Get off me, you pervy sheep! Ew! I have sheep poop on my jeans!"

"Emily, are you all right?"

"Yeah, but I'm all covered in gross mud and poop! That sheep right there stepped on me. On purpose! Boy, I hope Alec makes a nice roast of sheep out of you, buster!" I sat up and glared at the sheep as Holly skidded over to where I had fallen.

The sound of a whistle came from over the top of the hill. We both looked up. Sheep started flowing over the top like a wave of dirty gray and white.

"Crap, they're coming. Help me up; I have to gather my sheep. Where are yours?"

Holly pointed toward the far end of the field near the

gate, where a small huddle of sheep stood with Rob lying in the grass next to them.

"Wonderful. You get those two down there over to your group, and I'll get the rest. Ugh! I'm going to take the longest bath in the history of the world once I get those sheep."

Luckily, Lass is a natural herder, and she kept most of the remaining sheep together. The only two commands I could remember were *come bye* and *way to me*, but that does nothing for making the sheep go toward a gate. Alec didn't tell me the command for "make them go over to the gate and hurry up; the others are coming."

I ran around until I was behind them, and started jumping up and down, yelling and waving my arms, figuring if I started them in the right direction, then Lass could *come bye* and *way to me* them into a circle that moved toward the gate, and everything would be hunky-dory, and I could go soak in the tub with my vanilla-and-lavender sugar scrub and a copy of Paris *Vogue*.

Why is it that stuff never goes right for me? No, seriously, I'd like to know. Why doesn't the simplest thing go right for me?

There was one sheep, the one who trampled all over me when I was on the ground, who refused to go toward the gate.

"You stupid sheep," I said, running toward him. He turned around and ran in the other direction (opposite the gate), and since Lass was busy with the other three, which . . . um . . . had scattered as soon as they saw me jump up and down and wave my arms, it was clearly up to me to grab the problem sheep and drag it over to the stupid gate.

Here's another sheep fact: they're strong. If you happen to tackle one in midflight as it's running in the wrong direction, throwing your jacket over its head so you can make a leash out of your sleeves, they can drag you along the ground for thousands of miles before they finally stop.

"It's not funny," I yelled at Ruaraidh as he and Alec stood at the top of the hill and howled with laughter. I got to my feet, keeping one hand firmly on my jacket, which was twisted around the sheep's neck, and looked down at myself. I was covered in mud and sheep poop. Major ick! There was mud down my wellies, mud soaked through my jeans, mud under my sweatshirt, and I smelled like a sheep! "You have retarded sheep, Alec. This one attacked me! I demand that you kill it! It's rabid or something!"

Ruaraidh actually had to bend down and grab his legs, he was laughing so hard. I looked over to Holly, who stood with my two sheep next to her four. She had her hand over her mouth, pretending she was coughing, but I knew better.

"Oh, yes, it's very funny to see a poor, innocent American ravaged by packs of wild sheep!" I jerked my jacket tighter around the sheep's neck and started dragging him forward. He made a nasty sort of coughing/bleating sound, but I wasn't falling for that old "you're strangling me" trick. If I let go of him, he'd just knock me down again. "You're coming with me, buster, and if you know what's good for you, you'll behave—Ow! You stepped on my foot! That's it, you're dinner!"

It took me a good ten minutes to drag that stupid sheep over to where the others were. Holly offered to help, but by that time I had something to prove to the ha-ha boys with their gazillions of obedient sheep and their smug "told you so" looks.

"There," I said triumphantly (and muddily, but I refuse to think about that, because as you know, a major part of being truly coolio is maintaining the attitude of "nothing is ever wrong with me" no matter how bad things really are). "Here's my herd of sheep, Alec. Now, can I go have a bath?"

By that time both he and Ruaraidh had stopped laughing, although I saw Alec's shoulders shaking a lot like he was trying to hold it in.

"Eh . . . we've still the dosin' to do, lass, but if you'd rather go in . . ."

I looked at Ruaraidh. He was chatting with Holly, who was smiling up at him. She wasn't covered in sheep poop and mud, she didn't smell like a sheep, and she had no trouble controlling her group of four-legged sweaters on the hoof.

Rats. That means she gets another ten points. I ground my teeth for a bit while I weighed the benefits of a lovely hot bath with time spent impressing Ruaraidh with my totally fabulous sheep skills.

"No," I told Alec, heroic in the face of my duty. I'm brave that way. "I'll do the dosing first."

"Good lass. Brae, Rob, walk up."

It took a good forty-five minutes with Alec and Ruaraidh and all the dogs (not to mention me and Holly stumbling along behind) to get the sheep into the field next to the barn where they were to be dosed. We stopped for a brief lunch (I washed off as much muck as I could, and tried to sterilize my hands with what I thought was antibiotic soap until Alec told me it was salve for the goats' udders), and then went right into the dosing part of the day.

"I hate sheep," I muttered to myself as I followed when the guys went around the back of the barn. "I hate sheep, and I hate Scotland, and the only reason I'm staying is . . . Oh, hi, Ruaraidh! Long time no see."

He smiled (nice smile, bonus points to me for getting a smile just for saying hi). "Are you ready to dose the sheep?"

"Sure, been looking forward to it all day." Yes, yes, that was an outright lie, but it was a *kind* lie, so it doesn't count. "So . . . um . . . what do we do for this dosing thingy, give them a pill or something?"

He looked at me kind of funny. "You've never seen a sheep drenched?"

"Oh, sure I have. It was raining yesterday, and they really looked soaked."

He started to laugh, then put his arm around my shoulders as we walked to the rear of the barn. He put his arm around me!!! That means he likes me, right? Or do you think it was a sympathy thing? No, I'm sure it wasn't; I'm sure it was a guy-girl thing, because he didn't give me the Pity Look.

Go, me!

"It's not quite the same thing, Emily. Drenching is what we call dosing a sheep."

"Oh," I said, überly cool, just walking along with his arm around my shoulders. Arm on shoulders, that's got to be worth fifteen points, don't you think? Yeah, so do I. "It sounds . . . uh . . . wet."

"It's not particularly, unless you don't know how to use a drenching gun."

Well, poop, how was I supposed to know I had to take a class in basic sheep firearms before coming to Scotland?

As it turns out, the drenching gun isn't really a gun at all; it's a yellow thing with a long shiny nozzle thing and a hose thing, and stuff squirts out of it when you pull back on the trigger. Alec gave me a drenching gun, and showed me how to use it. It looked pretty simple—the dose of the gucky drenching stuff was set automatically, so all I had to do was stick the long shiny part in the sheep's mouth, squirt, and move on to the next sheep.

That sounds simple, but the sad truth is that sheep are not only stupid and mean; they also don't like having long shiny nozzle things stuck in their mouth. And let me just say, if anyone ever told me the day would come that I'd be standing out in a muddy pasture with a gazillion dirty, stinking, mean, selfish sheep who don't want to take their medicine, I'd have told them to get themselves a new brain, because this girl doesn't do that sort of thing, but there I was.

The sheep were squeezed through a long narrow fence area called—for some reason, don't try to figure it out, this is Scotland—a race. It makes the sheep go in single file, so you can drench them and stuff. Anyhoo, Holly was given driving duty, so she had to get the sheep through the race. Alec, Ruaraidh, and I hung out along the sides, and when a sheep stopped in front of us, we were supposed to insert the shiny thing, squeeze, and remove it for the next sheep.

"Alec!" I yelled when my first sheep refused to open its mouth. "What do you say to make them open their mouth?"

"You don't say anythin'," he answered.

I put my hands on my hips and gave him the Eyebrow of Fwah. "Well, then, how do you get the drenchy stuff in?"

He sighed and came over to where I was standing with my (obstinate and very stinky) sheep. "Look, you just slide it into her mouth like this, then pull the trigger. It's very easy."

I waved my nozzle at him. "I tried that, but the stupid thing just clamped its teeth together so I couldn't— Oh! Sorry about that, Alec."

Alec wiped the drenching stuff off his face, gave me a

look that didn't seem too happy, and went to the hose. Evidently the drenchy stuff is bad for people.

Oops!

He came back and stood next to me while I tried to drench the sheep, but she kept moving her head and bucking and stuff, and the next thing I knew, I'd drenched the fence, one of the dogs, my shoe, the sheep's butt, and Alec's left knee.

"It's not my fault!" I said when he took my drenching gun away from me, claiming I was a maniac with it. "It has a hair trigger! You just look at the thing and it squirts!"

Ruaraidh came back from where he was washing the drenchy off Kaylee. He wasn't smiling. In fact, he looked a bit cheesed at me. I don't know why; it was an accident! And it's not like I got him in the eye, like I did Alec.

I was demoted to sheep handler, and went to help Holly shove sheep into the race.

"I've changed my mind," Alec said, his face grim after he'd had to help us with the sheep for the fifth time. Honestly, Dru, the little buggers hate me! Every time I tried to get them into the race, they *baaaa*ed and ran around like mad, a one of them so demented it ran into the side of the barn and knocked itself silly. "I want my records computerized. You can do that instead of helpin' us with the sheep."

I looked over to where Ruaraidh was herding the staggering sheep toward the race. He wouldn't even look at me (Ruaraidh, not the sheep—it was in no state to see straight, silly), which means all my bonus points were taken away! Poop!

This calls for a drastic reevaluation of my life.

The bad: I won't be spending my days with Ruaraidh.

The good: I've seen the sorts of stuff Holly will be doing—I don't have to worry about her getting ahead in the point count with Ruaraidh. Mud and sheep poop and smelly wild animals just do not make for a romantic situation.

Also good: I've been promoted to computer work! That should look totally fabu on my résumé, huh?

So that's it, that's how my first day of work experience has gone. Day one: promotion! Can the conquering of Ruaraidh be far behind? I think not!

Point total—Holly: 25, Me: 15 (points taken away for drenching incidents). Don't go feeling bad for me, though. I'm v. confident I can make those points up.

I have to get ready for After Dinner TV Watching Time with Ruaraidh. Holly came in a while ago and went to take a bath, which means she's going to get all dressed up in an attempt to sway Ruaraidh with her womanly charms, and *that* makes it of vital importance that I outdress and out-womanly charm her.

Piece of cake!

Hey, speaking of cake, how did Timothy's birthday party go? Tell all. Did you guys get all busy with each other?

Hugs and computerized kisses,
~Em

Subject: re: Hiya, Fang!
From: Mrs.Legolas@kiltnet.com
To: Fbaxter@oxfordshire.agricoll.co.uk
Date: 4 January 2004 3:47pm

Fbaxter wrote:
> Sounds like you're having fun up there, even if it is muddy
> fun. We learned about Fluke last semester; it's a bad dis-

> ease. And yes, I've seen sheep dogs work; they are amaz-
> ing, aren't they? Who's this shepherd Holly has a pash
> on?

Um . . . just a guy, you know?

Oh, hey, Fang, get this—I'm learning how to knit! I'll knit you a sweater if you like, something to keep you all warm and toasty when you're doing your vet stuff at the stables. Send me your measurements, 'kay?

Oh, oh, oh! I almost forgot! You remember how you said that you and Devon might drive up here one weekend to see us? Well, Aunt Tim says there's a big celebration on the twenty-fifth, the birthday of this guy Robert Burns. He was a poet or something. I guess they have fireworks and stuff, although why anyone would want to celebrate the birthday of a poet is beyond me.

Anyway, if you and Devon can come up on that weekend, Aunt Tim says she read in the paper that there's going to be a circus in Inverness then—it's called Circus of the Darned. Sounds like fun, huh? Problem is, sleeping space is kinda nonexistent. There's only our room, and Ruaraidh's room, but that has only one bed. AT said you and Devon could sleep on the couches, though, so let me know.

I've only been gone five days and I already miss you guys! Tell me how your classes are going, and whether that colt with the hurt leg is all right. You know how I worry.

Big smoochy kisses,
Emily

Subject: re: Yuck on the sheep poop
From: Mrs.Legolas@kiltnet.com
To: Dru@seattlegrrl.com
Date: 4 January 2004 3:55pm

Dru wrote:
> I don't see how he can be a Scottish god of love if he
> thinks you're a boob, Em. I know you're maintaining and
> you're as cool as ever, but sheesh! Squirting his dog with
> that ucky stuff is not coolio.

   Maybe not, but it really wasn't my fault if the drenching
gun was wonky. And Ruaraidh was very smiley at dinner,
but that might have something to do with the fact that Holly
asked for his measurements so she could knit him a sweater.
   He *really* likes sweaters.
   Aunt Tim had a book on knitting, so when we went into
town to scope out the shops (pitiful, let me tell you!), Holly
and I stopped in at a yarn place and bought yarn and knitting needles. Holly looked at all sorts of needles and stuff,
talking to the store people about which kind were best for
knitting a sweater, but I didn't mess with any of that. I found
a cool pair of steel-blue knitting needles, which look really
good with the yarn I picked out. It's bluey-greeny with bits
of stuff twisted through it. V. pricey, and took up the rest
of my money from Brother, but Ruaraidh is worth it.
   Besides, Aunt Tim gave me fifty pounds as an early birthday pressie. Sweet, huh? I'm saving it for Inverness, which
is the nearest big town, one that has an actual mall! I'm
chuffed (*chuffed* means *thrilled*, BTW. Don't say *chuffing*,
though,'cause that means you've got gas. Is English slang
the weirdest on earth, or what?).

Now, tell me if this doesn't mean I'm on a certain Scottish god of love's top-ten list: Ruaraidh told he would teach me to drive! Yeah, yeah, I know you know I know how to drive—after all, I did scream through the driver's test back home, everything but that stupid parallel parking, which ought to be illegal anyway, because who wants to park if you don't have a proper parking spot with lines and everything?

Anyhoodles, at dinner last night—during which I was looking utterly fabu, of course, wearing my black vinyl micromini and red see-through shirt that made Ruaraidh's eyes bulge out when he saw me—at dinner Aunt Tim said it wasn't hard to learn how to drive on the left side of everything, even with the stuff in the car all turned around. "Maybe Alec would show you. You already have your license, so it shouldn't be that hard for you to learn."

"Ooooh," I said, eyeing Alec. "That would be v. fabu! Then I could drive myself around and wouldn't have to bother you guys."

"No," Alec said, rubbing the welt on the side of his neck where I accidentally whapped him with the drenching gun when he was trying to disentangle my leg from where it was caught up in the drenching hose thingy. "I think I'll be passin' on the opportunity to teach you how to drive my car. It's only a year old."

I started a pout, but didn't have a chance to get it warmed up before Ruaraidh said, "I'll teach you, Emily. It's legal for you to drive here, isn't it?"

Brother said he and Mom had to get some sort of international driving permit, but since they got it from a travel company, it can't be that important, right? "Sure, it is! I'm a very good driver, too."

"I'd like to come," Holly said quickly.

"You're too young to drive," I pointed out, then turned back to Ruaraidh. "I only failed parallel parking on my driver's test, and that was because the woman testing me was allergic to my perfume and spent the whole time with her head hanging out of the window."

"It would be educational for me to go with you." We all looked at Holly. She blinked really fast for a couple of seconds. "Well, it would be! I could watch how Emily does things, and . . . learn."

I gave her a squinty-eyed look, but she didn't look worried like she normally does when I do that. In fact, she bared her teeth at me in return, which kind of shocked me, because she's usually so nice. Sheesh! *Someone* is taking this competition thing a bit too seriously! "Thank you, Ruaraidh, I'd like it v. much if you'd show me. It would be totally cool if I could drive, because then I won't have to bother you guys when Holly and I want to go shopping or looking at castles and stuff."

"Castles?" Alec said, giving Aunt Tim a narrow-eyed look. "Don't tell me you've infected Emily with your lust for castles, love?"

He always calls her *love*. Isn't it sweet? I know, they're old and all, but I still think it's kind of cool the way they look at each other. Alec *does* have that scrummy accent, and I saw him without his shirt this morning when he was coming out of the bathroom—slobbersville! If I didn't like my aunt Tim so much, and didn't have a majorly huge hottie begging to do things like teach me how to drive in a lefty car, I'd have to think seriously about Alec.

"Being a castle junkie isn't a disease, Alec," Aunt Tim said, doing a little eye-flirty thing at him. "The girls are simply showing their natural good taste and intelligence with the desire to see the castles of Scotland, and if there happens to be a man or two standing around in a kilt while they're seeing the castles, well, so much the better! They'll get culture and history at the same time!"

Aunt Tim has a thing for guys in kilts, too. Good taste runs in my family.

Oh, and I know what you're thinking—castles? The very cool and hip Emily interested in moldy oldies? Yeah, well, all I can say is after last Halloween, when I saw Devon in his knight's costume, I've had a bit of a thing for castles and stuff like that. Which, I have to admit, makes having a father who's a medieval scholar a handy thing, because he gave me a book showing all of the castles of England and Scotland. Aunt Tim said she'd be happy to take us to as many castles as we could easily drive to, which is v. cool.

Back to dinner. Alec just groaned at Aunt Tim's happy, perky castle talk, and rubbed his neck welt again. "You'll be expectin' me to accompany you on these castle tours, won't you?"

"Of course," Aunt Tim said. "What's the use in being married to a romantic, dishy Scot in romantic, dishy Scotland if he doesn't take you through the local castles and tell you all about them?"

"I'm a sheep farmer, Tim, not a bleedin' historian. I don't know anythin' about castles."

"I do," I said, giving Ruaraidh a meaningful look. After all, if Aunt Tim had her dishy Scot to take her around the castles, it was only fair that I (oh, all right, Holly and *I*) should have a lickalicious Scottish love god. "Brother gave me a guidebook to all the castles in the area. It tells everything about them. You just take us to the ickle beasties, and we'll do the rest!"

I smiled at Ruaraidh. He looked a bit startled at first, then smiled back. "Ickle beasties?"

"I'm going Scottish," I explained.

"Ah. I've always found castles to be verra interesting."

I love how he says *very*. It's soooooooooo sexy!

I let him have my good smile, the one I save for special occasions. Thank heavens I was wearing my sparkly lip gloss—it can turn any smile into a dazzler. "Good, then you'll come with us. Now, let me see. . . ." I ran into the sitting room, where I'd left my PDA, bringing it to the dining table as I flipped through the calendar. "Er . . . tomorrow I'll be busy setting up Alec's sheep database, but I'm free on Tuesday. Can we go to a castle then?"

"Ooooh, yes," Holly said, her eyes lighting up. Before she met Ruaraidh she was going to be a teacher, so she really gets into historical things, and even has a sword, which, I have to admit, is pretty cool, but it's still a shame to see a perfectly nice girl like her with lots of coolio potential go to waste on historical stuff. "I would love to go to Urquhart Castle. It's not too far from here, is it?"

Side note: Urquhart—I had to look up the spelling. It's pronounced "irk hart." I think it's worth like a gazillion points in Scrabble.

"Urquhart! What a lovely idea," Aunt Tim said.

"It isn't," Alec said, his lips making a thin line. "Loch Ness in the middle of winter is anythin' but lovely, Tim. It'll be freezin' on the loch."

Loch is *lake* in Scottish. Or Gaelic (which, incidentally, is pronounced "GAL-lick," rather than "GAY-lick"). Either way, *loch* means *lake*.

(You know, I think I ought to get extra credit just for having to learn a whole new language here. It's only fair for making me learn things like how to say Gaelic, and the difference between *chuffed* and *chuffing*.)

Aunt Tim made pouty lips at Alec. "You can wear your sheepskin coat; you'll be nice and warm in it. Tuesday is fine with me, Emily. We'll all go, and make a day of it."

Alec grumbled something under his breath about harvesting turnips. We all pretended not to hear him.

"You'll like Urquhart," Ruaraidh told Holly and me. "I've been there many times."

Holly and I grinned at each other; then we turned to smile at Ruaraidh.

"Fantabulous," I said, thinking about how romantic it would be to kiss him in a real, authentic old-time castle. "You can be our tour guide and show us all the v. cool spots like the dungeons and the dark, secretive rooms where they used to sacrifice the virgins, and other fabu stuff."

"If I were you, lad," Alec told him, eying Holly and me, "I'd stay away from the dark, secretive virgin-sacrifice rooms, and stick to the wide-open spaces, where you'll be safe."

I blinked at Alec. He wasn't making any sense. Old people get that way. It's a shame, really, because other than his mind going, he is still droolworthy . . . in an older-man sort of way.

"Erm . . . where *the girls* will be safe, that is," he added, winking at Aunt Tim. "From rats and the like."

I wrinkled up my nose. Rats! Ew to the third power!

Tomorrow is our trip to Urquhart Castle, yay! This morning I started work on Ruaraidh's sweater, but I think something is wrong with Aunt Tim's knitting book, or the directions have to be translated because I'm from the U.S. or something, because so far all I have is a long line of knots on my pretty steel-blue knitting needle. I don't see how I'm supposed to double back on the knots, you know, the actual *knitting* part. It just keeps going on and on and on. I'm going to wait until Holly is taking her bath, then look at what she's done. She's got like four inches already! Meh!

So, enough about me; tell me what happened when you and Heather went to the Love Shoppe. Did they throw you out, like that time you and I snuck in and laughed at all the vibrating things? Did you see the wombat-fur nipple covers that I told you about? If they're not too expensive, could you pick me up a pair and send them to me? It's cold here; I think fur nipple covers might come in handy.

Hugs and kisses,
~Em

Subject: I have pig eyes!
From: Mrs.Legolas@kiltnet.com
To: Dru@seattlegrrl.com
Date: 4 January 2004 7:07pm

I was in the bathroom after dinner, and I looked in the mirror, and I just realized that I have teeny, tiny, squinty little piggy eyes! OMG! What am I going to do?

There's nothing to do but keep my eyes opened up really wide all the time.

Hugs and kisses,
~Em

Subject: Pig Eyes, Part Two
From: Mrs.Legolas@kiltnet.com
To: Dru@seattlegrrl.com
Date: 4 January 2004 7:19pm

I just went downstairs to see what everyone was doing, and Aunt Tim asked me if I'd seen a ghost or something.

"Huh?" I asked.

"Your eyes are bugging out like you've seen something frightening," she said.

Bugging out? Wah! I hate my eyes!

Bug-eyed hugs and kisses,
~Em

Subject: re: That editor is *so* screwed!
From: Mrs.Legolas@kiltnet.com
To: Dru@seattlegrrl.com
Date: 6 January 2004 9:12pm

Dru wrote:
> and when I got the copy of my article back, the editor—
> Sue Mallory, you remember her—had changed the word
> *God* to *Crod*! She said it was a spellchecker error. Isn't
> that too funny? OHMICROD! Hahahahahahahah!

Well, first off, where does Sue M. come off editing your article? It's the school newspaper, for Pete's sake, not Salon.com or the *Seattle Times* or something! And since your article was about freedom of speech and censorship, I think it's really wrong for her to be changing stuff around. And spellchecker error? What kind of word is *Crod* that it would change it to that? I think she changed it just so you'd look stupid!

But yeah, that is a hoot. Crod! Heh heh heh.

Glad you guys had fun at the naughty shop. I miss doing stuff like that with you! I have Holly here, but she's just not the "run into an adult shop and mock the vibrating things" kind of girl, you know what I mean? Anyway, I'm not going to say anything bad about her despite her being waaaaaay too competitive over Ruaraidh, because she showed me what was going wrong with my knitting last night, and didn't once say anything about why I couldn't seem to stop knitting one long chain of knots, even though she must have known that I had fibbed a bit about knowing how to do it.

And speaking of Holly, I've been thinking about her. I've told you what she's like—she's very shy, and doesn't talk much, and is kind of intimidated by stuff, so this business with her talking more and volunteering to do things with Ruaraidh is definitely out of character. Maybe being around me has made her more self-confident? I hope so; she really is nice and her coolio rating is definitely on the rise.

> The castle thing sounds . . . well, I have to say, Em, it
> doesn't sound very you. I mean, castles are old! They're
> historical! I hate to say it, but they're downright geeky! I'd
> hate for you to be seen somewhere geeky; it just isn't
> good for your reputation.

You know, I used to think that too, but man-o-rama, Dru, if you'd seen Devon last year in his knight costume . . . *fans self*. And Ruaraidh likes castles, so even if they were geeky normally, they're mondo über-coolio when you've got an eleven-fingered Scottish god of love showing you around.

Oh, BTW, you asked what he does for gloves—I checked. He shoves his extra pinkie in with the other one. I can't help but wonder what it would be like to hold hands with him. I mean, what does the extra finger do?

So, on to the good stuff. We went to Urquhart today. Now, I have to say, when I go to see a castle, I expect there to be a castle there to see, not just ruins, which is what Urquhart was. It's on Loch Ness (yes, the place with Nessie, although that's really just all silliness if you ask me—if there really was a Nessie, Steven Spielberg would have found her by now), and Alec was right; it was colder than a witch's tit there.

Ohmicrod, said the T-word! Hee!

The first thing we saw when we got there was a visitor's center with a gift shop and café (I bought some very cool heather soap for you, because I know you like smelly soaps). Alec went off to use the men's room while we looked around.

"Brr, a bit cold out this morning," Ruaraidh said, rubbing his arms.

"Would you like a cup of tea?" Holly asked. "I'll get you one if you'd like."

He smiled at her (five points). "No, thank you."

"I'd like a big cup of very hot coffee," Aunt Tim said, wrapping her scarf around her neck. "One big enough I can soak in. Emily, you must be freezing in that short skirt."

"Nope, warm as can be," I said, despite the fact that I really was a Popsicle on legs. That didn't matter; what did was Holly's attempt to shove her way up in the points by offering to get Ruaraidh a cup of tea. "How about something to eat, Ruaraidh? Hungry, hmmm? I'd be happy to go to the café for you."

"No, thank you," Ruaraidh said to me, giving me the same smile he gave Holly. Goal!

"If you're going to the café, could you get me some coffee?" Aunt Tim asked, blowing on her gloves and stomping her feet.

"How about some sweets?" Holly asked.

"It doesn't have to be a big cup of coffee, just so long as it's warm," Aunt Tim said.

"Chockies!" I said brightly. "What a great idea. I'll just run along and get you some! Who wants to see a castle without chocolates to munch on?"

"I'm not much of one for sweets," Ruaraidh told us.

"A cup of hot water would do in a pinch."

"Maybe you'd like a commemorative T-shirt," Holly said, eyeing the gift-shop window.

"No, thank you, I don't—"

"Oooh, look, they have plaid stuff!" Two could play Holly's little game, bwahahahah. "Tell you what, Ruaraidh, since you're going to the trouble of being our tour guide, I'll treat you to a plaid thing. How about a nice scarf?"

"That's very thoughtful of you, but—"

"Room-temperature water would even be welcome at this point."

"What you need is a Nessie," Holly said, pointing to a stuffed toy. "Just a little something so you can remember this visit. The sign says you can have it personalized—we could have our names and the date put on it."

Oh! That rat! She wouldn't!

"What's the matter, love?" Alec asked as he came up to us. "You look fair fashed."

"Coffee," Aunt Tim answered in a weak little voice. "Hot coffee. Please, if you have any love for me, take me to coffee."

"Whatever you like." Alec turned to follow Aunt Tim to the café, pausing in front of me. "Is everthin' all right, lass?"

I blinked at him. "What?"

"You look a wee bit startled. Is somethin' the matter?"

I muttered, "No, nothing," and glared at Holly when she snickered (she knows about my tiny eyes).

We walked around the upper part of the castle while Aunt Tim had her coffee. I have to say, I wasn't terribly impressed with the castle. It was mostly ruins, just a bunch of stone walls and bumps and hilly grass things, and a lot of dirt and broken stones and stuff. According to Ruaraidh, the place was blown up to keep some Scottish guys from taking it over, which is just silly because it's in Scotland! Of course Scottish guys are going to be here!

Just looked it up in Brother's book. Jacobites, that's what the Scottish dudes were called (a cult who worshiped a guy named Jacob?). Oh. Wait. The book says the Jacobites wanted some king named James II to be king of Scotland and England after he got kicked out during a revolution. How did they get *Jacobites* from James, that's what I want to know. Anyway, once Aunt Tim and Alec came out of the café, we wandered around for a bit, and Ruaraidh read stuff out of Brother's book about what things were, and what the castle used to be like, but it wasn't too thrilling until we saw the piper.

I know what you're thinking—first castles, now bagpipes; where is this going to end? Before you start scrunching up your nose at the thought of bagpipes, let me point out that where there's a bagpipe, there's usually a guy in a kilt.

"Kilt!" I bellowed, and pointed when I saw the piper guy standing at the base of the tower house.

"Where?" Aunt Tim said, pushing Alec aside. Holly was right with her.

"There. Isn't he nummy?"

Alec snorted something rude behind us.

"Dibs the first picture with him," I said, and started running down the path toward the big tower, Holly right on my heels.

Here's the thing: it's been cold here. Not snowing, but freezing. Today it was sunny, but still really cold. Now, you've had chemistry; combine cold weather and wet spray from the loch with a cobblestone path, and what do you get? That's right, you get frost and ice!

I am here to tell you that frosty cobblestones and very stylish, totally tight chunky shoes do not mix well. Just as I ran into a long, shaded dip in the pavement directly in front of the piper, I hit a patch of black ice and fell. On my knees.

Skinning them.

In front of Ruaraidh *and* the piper guy.

Can I die now?

"Emily!" Holly shrieked, right in my ear because she was hauling me up to my feet. "Are you all right?"

"Well, I'm going to be deaf in my left ear, but yeah, I think so."

"Don't move!" Ruaraidh yelled down from where he was standing near the upper gate. "I've had first-aid training!"

First aid? Yay! I collapsed back down onto the ground, shoving Holly out of the way so Ruaraidh could take me in his strong, manly arms and save me. "Oh! The pain! Oh! My knees! Oh!"

OK, OK, so it wasn't the most brilliant thing to say; you

try to come up with something fabu when you've just fallen down and skinned your knees like you're a six-year-old.

"Emily!" Holly whispered to me. "You ought to be ashamed of yourself!"

"If you're not ashamed by offering to buy Ruaraidh a Nessie with your names embroidered on it, I'm not ashamed about this," I hissed back at her.

"Are you hurt?" The piper set down his bagpipes and ran over to squat next to me. "That was a nasty tumble you took."

"Right in front of Ruaraidh, too. How curious," Holly said, in a jaded sort of voice. She gave me a look that just came right out and said she thought I'd fallen down on purpose. As if!!!

I ignored her and gave the piper a quick once-over, and decided that although he was very cool in his kilt and a pretty ruffled shirt, he was too old for me. I smacked at his hand when he tried to feel around my kneecap.

"Go away!" I said through my teeth so Ruaraidh wouldn't hear as he ran up to me.

"Your knees could be seriously hurt—"

"No, they're not! Please go away! As in, like, *now*!"

Ruaraidh knelt beside me, and sucked in his breath as he looked at my scraped knees. "Ouch. That'll sting, I'll wager."

"She's done both of them," the piper said helpfully.

I gave him a three-second scowl before turning to Mr. Hottie. "Oh, Ruaraidh, thank God you're here!"

Holly snorted. *Snorted!* What's next for her, saying that "tch" thing that old people do?

"We're here, too," Aunt Tim said. She and Alec had followed Ruaraidh, and now they all stood around looking down at me.

"How lucky I am that you've had first-aid training," I told Ruaraidh. Hey, I'm not stupid! I might not have fallen down on purpose, but I sure as shootin' was going to take advantage of all my pain and suffering.

"Alec knows lots of medical things because of the animals. Don't you, sweetie?"

"Lots," Alec said, peering over Ruaraidh's shoulder to look at my legs. "Ouch."

"An expert opinion is always a good thing to have," I pointed out.

"Oh, Alec's had lots of experience patching up the animals."

"Expert *human* experience," I said, with emphasis.

"Hmmm," Ruaraidh said as he bent over my knees.

"How bad do you think I'm hurt? Will I be able to walk? Maybe *someone* should help me to my feet?" I didn't exactly bat my eyelashes at Ruaraidh, but they were definitely fluttering in the wind.

"Emily, I tried, but you wouldn't let me——" Holly started to say.

"Here, let's get you up, then," the piper interrupted Holly, and grabbed my arm.

"Ack!" I yelled, and swooned over sideways onto Ruaraidh.

Or I would have if he had still been there, but he was standing in order to help the piper pull me up, so I ended up swooning over sideways into the frosty mud.

"Of all the——ack, pooh!——rotten tricks," I said, spitting out mud and grass and gravel.

"Sorry," Ruaraidh said as he helped me up. "I didn't know

you were going to do that. How do you feel?"

"Faint," I said, weaving a little. Toward him, you understand. "Must be the blood loss. Maybe you should do mouth-to-mouth."

I made sure my eyes were open really wide when I said it, because no one wants to do mouth-to-mouth on a girl with little pig eyes.

"Erm . . . I don't think that's necessary," Ruaraidh said. "Did you get some dirt in your eye when you fell?"

"No," I said.

"Ah, good. The way your eyes were bulging, I thought you might have."

That's it. I give up. I'm just doomed to having tiny little slits for eyes.

Aunt Tim made a half snort, half laugh. I have no idea why; there wasn't anything funny about me having horribly small eyes, but I've noticed she laughs a lot for no reason. Alec muttered something about seeing if the gift shop had some eyewash, then hauled Aunt Tim off to see the water gate. The piper went back to stand next to the drawbridge to the tower house.

Ruaraidh looked down at my legs. I have to say, despite the cold and my skinned-up knees, I'm really glad I wore my short skirt, because he was doing a whole lot of looking at my legs, and you *know* that has to be a good thing. "You're not bleeding, Emily; your knees are just scraped a bit raw. Once you clean them up, they should be fine. Do you feel up to walking around the rest of the castle?"

"Meh!" I said, and collapsed into his arms, which, if I say so myself, was a v. cool move. Have you ever tried to collapse into a guy's arms? It's not easy. I mean, if you collapse too hard, you could knock the other person down, which is definitely not a good thing. On the other hand, you want to make him think he needs to support you; otherwise he'll just prop you up and let go. And then there's the arms—where do you put your arms when you're collapsing? I decided to fling mine around Ruaraidh's neck, which turned out to be lucky, because he wasn't expecting me to throw myself at him, and he staggered backward for a few steps before he grabbed me.

"Erm," he said.

"Emily!" Holly said, sounding all outraged and stuff.

"You smell nice," I told Ruaraidh, because I think it's important to make people feel good about themselves. "Are you wearing aftershave? If you are, I really like it. Do you like my perfume? It's called Passion's Midnight Flower."

"Erm—"

"Emily!" Out of the corner of my eye I could see Holly dancing around, wringing her hands.

Heh heh heh.

"If you sniff behind my ear, you can smell it better," I said, turning my head so he could smell my neck.

"Eh—"

"Emily!" Holly's voice was sounding really desperate.

Ten points for me!

"It's very expensive, you know, but I've always felt that it was a mistake to go with cheap perfume. Who wants to smell like every other girl?"

Holly grabbed my arm. "If you're feeling so weak you have to cling like a bloodsucking leech to Ruaraidh, maybe you should go back to the car."

I glared at her for the leech comment. She made a little distressed gesture with her hands, as if she were really worried about me, and not the fact that I was in prime kissing position with the sexiest man in Scotland. "I'm sure your aunt and uncle wouldn't want you to risk serious injury by coming with us to see the tower house and all."

"Oh, I'm feeling much better now," I said, turning back to look at Ruaraidh. I was still slumped up against him, his arms loosely around my waist, my hands on his shoulders. I gave him my bright, perky smile. "I love Scotland so much, I wouldn't let anything keep me from seeing the sites, not even the near-fatal wounding of my knees."

"Er . . . good," he said.

I (reluctantly) pulled myself off of Ruaraidh, and started down the remainder of the path with Holly. My knees did hurt a little, but not that much, not enough to make me want to go back to the car while she hogged Ruaraidh. I was about to tell her that when she grabbed my arm and whispered, "That wasn't very subtle at all."

"Of course it was; subtle is my middle name," I whispered back. "And anyway, it was good for fifteen points, don't you think?"

"I think you're cheating," she said stubbornly.

"Ha! You're just jealous because he was holding me, not you. Come on; he's waiting for us. At least there's some part of this castle standing!"

The rest of the castle trip was OK. We climbed a very scary, very steep spiral staircase in the tower house—it's five stories tall—and halfway up Holly decided she was afraid of heights, and stood there whimpering pitifully until Ruaraidh, who was at the top with me looking out at the rest of the castle, came back down and helped her down to the ground floor.

Honestly, have you ever heard of anything so sneaky? Acting like she's scared just so she could nab Ruaraidh—what a poop! Um . . . we're going to ignore that whole thing with my knees and telling the R-man I needed mouth-to-mouth. 'Cause it was a totally different situation.

Kind of.

Gotta go. Big day tomorrow—Ruaraidh is taking me driving! Hoo, baby!

Hugs and kisses,
~Em

Subject: re: No, I am not buying you a car!
From: Mrs.Legolas@kiltnet.com
To: Hwilliams@mediev-l.oxford.co.uk
Date: 7 January 2004 8:19am

Hwilliams wrote:
> If you think I'm going to buy you a car for your birthday
> when we're leaving England in September, you're insane.
> I don't see why you need to drive when Timandra and
> Alec will take you wherever you need to go. Need I remind
> you that there are such things as laws? You need an
> international driver's permit to drive here, and *you* do not
> have one.

Isn't it your job as a parental unit to encourage me to do things that will make me independent and happy and well-adjusted and all that stuff? 'Cause if it is, you're failing. Let's look at the situation from a realistic point of view, shall we? You can either buy me a car here and let me drive it around for the next nine months, or you can pay for majorly intensive therapy for all the trauma you've caused me for years and years and years. It's your choice, Brother. I'm just trying to save you some money.

> You're not molesting that boy with the unpronounceable
> name, are you?

Excuse me, do I know you well enough to talk about personal and private things like my love life with you? I think not. Next subject!

> If I hear that you've been attempting to seduce the poor
> boy . . .

Talk to the hand, Brother.

Thine,
Emily

Subject: re: Those vibrating things
From: Mrs.Legolas@kiltnet.com
To: Dru@seattlegrrl.com
Date: 7 January 2004 8:58am

Dru wrote:
> were so funny, but the weirdest of all was the feathers!
> Have you ever heard of feathers being used for, you
> know, *it?*

Really? Feathers? Wouldn't that tickle? Is tickling sexy? Did I miss a "benefits of tickling" article in *YM*?

> How are your knees? I think that was totally clever of you
> to ask Ruaraidh to massage your legs after you got home.
> I don't care what Holly says; that wasn't cheating at all—it
> was just being resourceful. How is the Campaign to Snag
> the Schottie going? (Schottie=Scottish Hottie).

Schottie! Too cute! My knees are better. They really didn't
hurt too much yesterday, and today they're just ugly, so I'm
wearing jeans.

Today I'm working on Alec's sheep stuff, which, let me
tell you, is boring as all get-out. There are no pictures of the
sheep, and they don't have names, just numbers, and the
information is all about how much they weighed when they
were born, and who their moms and dads were, and
whether they were sold or kept for breeding. Dull, duller,
dullest!

I had this great idea to keep me from being bored doing
sheep stuff! You're going to die, it's *such* a fabu idea! I'm
going to set up a Web page!

No, no, no, not a boring old Web page like everyone has;
I'm going to set up an Emily's Hottie of the Week page!
Every week I'll put up a picture and bio of some utterly drool-
worthy guy, and girls everywhere will come to slobber on
him. I'm sure the Web page will be a total hit with everyone,
and I'll probably get written up in *People* magazine or something, and end up really famous, and get invited to movie
previews, where all the hotties will beg me to make them a
Hottie of the Week (HOTW! Coolio!).

Will send you the URL once I get the Web page designed
and the first Hottie up—who do you think it should be? I'm
leaning toward Orlando Bloom. After all, I *am* a Legolass,
and he *is* the *über*-hottie, so it's only right, don't you think?

> And as for Tim—I just don't know about him. I mean, he
> seems like he really likes me and all, but he's just so . . .
> *you know*. Geeklike. He can't wear contacts, he *likes*
> being part of the IT team (no offense—I know you are
> into technology and Web stuff as well), and he just
> seems . . . well, kind of immature when you compare him
> to other guys. I met this guy at my cousin Sam's party last
> weekend, and he's really into photography, and he asked
> if he could take my picture sometime, so I said yes, and
> he said he'd call me. It's been five days and he hasn't
> called! Do you think I should start panicking yet?

Well, first things first—I don't think Timothy is geekish;
he's just a bit . . . um . . . shy, if you know what I mean.
Ordinary. Not horribly exciting.

Oh, all right, he's as geeky as they come. But you know,
a boyfriend in hand is worth two in the bush and all that,
so before you go dumping him, you might want to be sure
that you have another BF lined up to take his spot. I can tell
you from actual real-life experience how horrible it is to
break up with a guy without having a guy friend support
system in place. I don't know what I would have done after
I dumped Aidan if Devon and Fang hadn't been there when
I needed them.

Now tell me more about this photographer guy? Name?
Age? College or high school? Hunkalicity factor? What does
he look like? What did he say to you? What did you say to
him? If it's someone Sam knows, is he into Goth stuff?
Pierced or a piercing virgin?

Five days is within the allowed seven-day period for a guy
to call, so I wouldn't start wigging out just yet. Wait until

Friday. If he hasn't called by Friday night, then you can freak. I wouldn't go to the trouble of having a good freakout until then.

Kisses and hugs,
~Em

Subject: re: HOTW?
From: Mrs.Legolas@kiltnet.com
To: Dru@seattlegrrl.com
Date: 7 January 2004 6:00pm

Dru wrote:
> Oooh! A Hottie of the Week page! I love it! What'll you
> have on it?

Just a quickie, because dinner is in a few minutes. Yes, the HOTW idea is utterly fabu, and I'm really excited about it. I did a little bit of work on it today, in between entering in stupid sheep facts. More about that later (the HOTW, not the stupid sheep facts).

> Driving with Ruaraidh? Hmm. Can we say "perfect op-
> portunity to get a little busy"?

You know, that's what I like about you; you think just like I do! Well, there's not really much to tell about the learning-to-drive biz. Ruaraidh took me out after lunch in his little Honda. It wasn't a stick, so that was good (do you know that Brother still yells at me for burning out the clutch in his MG? That was *so* a year ago!). Holly wanted to come, and she pinched me twice during lunch when I just happened to mention to Alec how much she enjoyed doing sheepy things, but in the end, Alec asked her to go with him to take care of a couple of hurt sheep, so I got Ruaraidh all to myself.

Go, me!

Ruaraidh showed me where everything was in the car—it's all backward!—and then gave me directions for driving around the area.

OK, I've mentioned that Alec and Aunt Tim live in the Highlands, right? They're in a real rural area, with lots of farms and stuff. The roads are OK, hilly but not scary or anything, and just perfect for driving on if you haven't driven in a car with everything switched around to the right side.

I toodled out of the farm and down the road, heading for the nearest town.

"Turn left there and that road will take us down past the Walkers' farm and into town," Ruaraidh said. "Erm . . . Emily, you're on the right."

"I know, I know," I said as I turned the corner (thank Crod there was no one there because I just *couldn't* turn left smack into the left lane). I have to say, it's really strange sitting on the wrong side of the car, driving on the wrong side of the road, but after Ruaraidh made me practice a few more turns (left seemed to be the worst), I was feeling pretty copacetic and decided that this was the perfect time to do a little guy/girl work.

"Alec says your dad used to be a cattle farmer, but now he's not?" I asked, checking the rearview mirror to make sure my lipstick (Jade Blossom Pink) wasn't all over my teeth. "Is that why you're working for him and not your dad?"

"Yes. My dad was hit hard by the hoof-and-mouth outbreak we had a few years ago," he said, looking really unhappy. Rats. Wrong thing to talk about. Minus three points. "He sold the farm and moved down south. Mum didn't want to leave the Highlands because she's lived here all her life, but they didn't have much choice."

"Oh. Sorry to hear that. So, um, do you have brothers and sisters?"

"One sister. She's a witch."

I laughed and gave him an understanding smile. "I know what you mean; my sister, Bess, is normally OK, but she can be a total witch when she wants."

"You're on the right again," he warned. Gah! I zoomed over to the left. "I wasn't talking about my sister's attitude; I meant it literally. She and Mum both are witches. Wiccans, they say."

OMC! His mom is a witch?!?

"Really? How fabu! Do they make up love spells and stuff?"

He drummed the fingers of his right hand on his thigh. I couldn't help but sneak little glances at both his thigh and his hand. He was in jeans again. What is it about jeans on a guy when he's sitting in a car next to you that makes them so sexy? I love the way his jeans hugged his thighs. It was so scrummy! The six fingers drumming away on the scrummy leg kind of threw me, though. "Sometimes, not often though. Mum says you can't make someone love you if it wasn't fated to be."

"Oh." I tried to think of something else to say, but all I could think to talk about was his extra finger or his thighs, and you know how hard it is to bring up the subject of thighs in normal guy/girl conversation. "So I'm going to be in England until September."

"Are you? Will you be sorry to be going home?"

"Oh, yeah, although I do miss my friends back home. My best friend, Dru, is there (see? I mentioned you to the Schottie!), and my other friend . . . uh . . . Rita."

Yes, yes, that's a lie—I know that you know that Rita is a total flake—but all of a sudden I had a totally brill idea! I figured the points I'd lose over lying to him (seven) would be more than made up with the bonus points I'd get when he was so overcome with appreciation for my really good qualities that he'd snog me silly.

"Rita's my second-best friend. She's got different-colored eyes, you know? One's brown, and the other is green. A lot of people make fun of her because of that, but I don't. I think it's wrong to pick on someone just because they're a bit odd. Different, I meant," I said, glancing quickly at his hand. "People like that can't help the way they are."

"That's very true," he said, but didn't seem to be too impressed with how noble and pure my soul was. Rats. I'd hate to think I'd wasted a good lie.

"Do you . . . um . . . get teased about your finger?"

He looked down at his hand, all surprised. "No, I don't. Turn right here, and that'll take you back toward the farm."

" 'Kay. Um. Good."

He looked at me kind of funny.

"I mean, it's good that you don't get teased about your finger. That would be just wrong, because it's not like you had a choice about it or anything."

"Does it bother you?" he asked, his head tipped on the side like a puppy dog's.

"Me? No! Not in the least! I don't think it's weird at all! Nope, I don't even think about it. In fact, I'd totally forgotten about it until just now."

He nodded and looked back out the window.

"But since you mentioned it, I was wondering if it's a thing in your family. You know, like a birthmark? My sister and father and I all have a birthmark on our backs shaped like a question mark, and Mom says it's got something to do with dominant genes and stuff like that. I just wondered if anyone else in your family has six fingers."

He smiled. "Most of them have ten."

OHMICROD! Ten fingers? On each hand??? Eeeek! How do they type?

"Ten fingers, you know?" He waggled the fingers of both hands at me. "I was making a joke, Emily."

"Oh, a joke! Hahahahahah! Ten fingers, I get it. Ha!"

"You're on the . . . There you go. Good girl, you're doing fine."

We drove along for a few minutes not saying anything, just listening to Moray Firth radio. (Moray Firth is a place, BTW. It's . . . uh . . . some sort of a firth. I think.) I chewed on my lip a bit, trying to think of stuff to say that would make him mad with lust for me, but it's hard thinking up stuff like that when you're sitting on the wrong side of a car, driving on the wrong side of the road, and there's a hottie with six fingers on his right hand sitting next to you.

"My dad wanted to have my finger cut off when I was born," Ruaraidh said suddenly. I glanced at him out of the corner of my eye. He was looking down at his hand, flexing his fingers. "But Mum wouldn't let him have the doctors do it. She said it was an omen, a sign that I'd be lucky throughout my life."

"Oh. Well, that's a v. cool way of thinking about it."

"My girlfriend thought it was a bit creepy, but to tell you the truth"—he shrugged—"I forget it's there most of the time."

Girlfriend? Alec said he didn't have a girlfriend! What's this about a girlfriend? Ack! "Well, she can't be much of a girlfriend if she thinks something about you is creepy. I would never think that about any of my BFs."

He smiled. "She's not my girlfriend anymore. We broke up a few months ago."

Whew!

"I'll bet you have lots of boyfriends, eh?"

"Me? Um . . . I just broke up with someone, too. A few months ago. He was a real creep. He tried to make me touch him . . . you know, *there*."

His eyebrow went up. "You don't like touching guys . . . *there*?"

Oh, Crod, now he was going to think I was totally immature! "Sheesh, no, I love it! I touch guys *there* all the time. Well, the ones that want me to. I mean, I wouldn't go touching some guy *there* if he didn't want me to; he's got to have, you know, wanted me to touch him. Because otherwise, I wouldn't."

I am an idiot. Yes, I know this will come as shock to you, Dru, but I was babbling like an idiot! I couldn't stop! Everything I said just made it all worse!

Ruaraidh stared at me like I had a boob growing off my forehead or something.

"It's not like I have a thing about guys' . . . um . . . *you know*. I'm not a perv or anything. I don't just go around grabbing guys' thingies whenever I feel like it. There's got to be mutual-interest stuff going on between us before I thingy-touch. Boy, this road sure is curvy, isn't it? Is that the road to Alec's house? Should I turn left there?"

He started laughing, and for a moment I wanted to die because I was sure he was laughing at me, but then he put his hand on my knee and squeezed it. A knee squeeze! Ka-ching! Twenty-five points! I couldn't wait to tell Holly. "I really like you, Emily. You've got a great sense of humor."

He likes me! He likes my sense of humor! Oh. Wait. Does that mean he thinks I'm goofy?

"I like you too, Ruaraidh," I said, giving him one of my shy, yet sexy smiles.

He gave my knee another squeeze, and pointed down the road a little bit. "Why don't you pull up over there, next to the fence?"

OMC! He wants to neck! Right here in his car! In front of a field of cows! Now, this is where experience is so valuable—I didn't go through all that crap I went through with Aidan for nothing! At long last I could use the things I learned: a) Aidan was a creep, and b) any guy who wanted you to thingie-touch is probably also a creep, unless he's been your BF for a long time and stuff like that.

I was just getting ready to tell Ruaraidh that although I liked him a whole lot, I wasn't going to do anything other than kissing, when he said, "I thought we'd work a bit on your parallel parking."

I pulled off onto the side of the road and blinked at him. He didn't want to make out? "What?"

"You said you failed parallel parking, so I thought you could practice it a bit now, since you're out learning how to drive on the left."

I blinked a couple more times. I know, I know, it's not the prettiest or smartest-looking move to make, but honestly, Dru, sometimes you just have to give in and blink. "You want me to park? You don't want to make out with me? That's why you had me pull over? So I could practice *parking*?"

71

He blinked right back at me. "Make out? Erm . . . Emily, I like you and all, but—"

"But what? But I have hideously small eyes and you don't want to kiss me, is that it?"

"No, of course not, I like your eyes—"

"Then why don't you want to make out with me? What's wrong with me? Is it my hair? It's my roots, isn't it—you don't like my roots? Well, I can't help that! I can't redye my hair or it'll all fall out, and you can take it from me that an Emily with roots is a whole lot prettier than a bald Emily!"

He started laughing again, then leaned over and kissed me on the cheek. "You really are something special, Emily. Now come on; let's get this done. I have to help Alec with the footbath. I'll stand just over there. Pretend I'm the back end of a car, and that tree leaning over the fence is another car, and park between us."

OK, I admit it, my mouth hung open just the teensiest bit as I watched him get out of the car. He kissed me! He thinks I'm something special! He squeezed my knee. Twice! But he didn't want to make out? *Gah!* Will I ever understand guys?

I'd like to point out that Ruaraidh is to blame for what happened next. I was rattled enough by the kiss and the knee squeezing, and being in a backward car, trying to park on the left side of the street, which is just *wrong*, so for him to expect me to be able to parallel-park in an infinitesimally small pretend parking spot was just too much.

I ran over his foot. By mistake, of course, but still, it was really all his fault, because if he had wanted to make out like he should have, then he wouldn't have been standing at the side of the road telling me he was the back end of a car, and waving me forward.

Alec took him to the hospital after I drove home. Ruaraidh didn't squeeze my knee any more, or say he liked me again, or much of anything, to be honest. He just kind of moaned. You know me, I'm supersensitive to people's emotions and stuff, and I sensed he was a bit cheesed over the fact that I broke his big toe.

You think this is going to affect our relationship?

Gotta run; dinner's on.

Hugs and kisses,
~Em

Subject: re: How's my ghost?
From: Mrs.Legolas@kiltnet.com
To: BessWill@btinternet.co.uk
Date: 8 January 2004 9:11am

Bess wrote:
> know why you think your room is haunted; I've never
> seen a ghost there, and you know how sensitive to creepy
> environments I am. Besides, if there was a ghost, why
> would it only haunt your underwear drawer, and not the
> whole room?

Because I've got a pervy ghost, that's why! Hey, do me a big favor. Holly says her mom's friend who is a psychic won't do séances anymore because she's been born again, so I need to find someone who will exorcise the ghost in my undies. You've got a bunch of weirdo friends—can you see if one of them will contact the ghost for me once I get back to England?

Ta ever so.

> Brother says you've got your eye on some guy up there
> who has eleven fingers. What's the story on that? I
> thought after Aidan you swore off guys for at least six
> months while you recovered from your broken heart?

Oh, well, you know how it is—girl meets kissalicious guy, guy tells girl he likes her, and then girl runs over guy's foot. In other words, sometimes these things just happen. Kiss-met, I think they call it. Whatever, it works for me!

Later, chicky,
Emily

Subject: re: What do you think? Does he really like me?
From: Mrs.Legolas@kiltnet.com
To: Dru@seattlegrrl.com
Date: 8 January 2004 3:40pm

Dru wrote:
> Why do guys say they're going to call you, but then they
> don't? I've got a report due tomorrow; doesn't he un-
> derstand that I can't possibly concentrate on stupid his-
> tory stuff if I'm too busy waiting for him to call? *Meh!* Why
> can't guys ever do what they say they're going to do???

Aw, Dru, I'm sorry Brent hasn't called by now. I was sure he would, because if someone asks if he can take your picture, that's serious. He wouldn't want your picture if he thought you were dorky or something, right? So he must be serious about you, even though you guys just met. That love-at-first-sight stuff is powerful!

Maybe he's sick, or a relative died and he had to fly off to go to the funeral, or his parents forgot to pay their phone bill, or he was abducted by aliens and they did weird experiments on him, and now he's too embarrassed about the brain implant to call you.

Just kidding about that last one, heh heh heh.

Well, *I* thought it was funny.

> You don't think he's changed his mind, do you? Is he
> trying to break up with me? OHMICROD, that's it, isn't
> it? He's dumping me! WAH!

Well, um . . . you guys weren't really together, so I don't see how he could break up with you, but in any case, no, I don't think he's dumping you. I think maybe he lost your phone number, or forgot your name or something stupid like that. But I don't think you're in the Dumpster.

Here, I have something to make you feel better—I've got the first Hottie of the Week done! Here's what it looks like:

Emily's Hottie of the Week
Hottie #1—Orlando Bloom!
(I'll put a picture of Orlando Bloom right here—the one of him in the red T-shirt where he's just barely smiling, and looks so nummy you want to eat him with a spoon and lick the bowl afterward. . . . Sorry, was Legolusting there for a few minutes.)

- Name: Orlando Bloom
- Birthdate: January 13, 1977
- Height: 5'11"
- Famous for: the hottest elf in all of Middle Earth

- Skateboarding skill: fabu!
- Can he shoot a bow and arrow: standing, riding, or sliding down stairs on shield (v. cool!)
- Does he look good in tights: oh, baybee!
- Does he look good in a blond wig: *swoon*
- Coolness rating: ten out of ten pointy ears
- Surf or motorcycle: surfing!
- Chest test (max amount you'd spend on a T-shirt with him on the front): $22
- Dream date: on the beach for a day of surfing and tanning, followed by a bonfire and romantic dinner as the sun sets, then a long walk on beach under the stars, holding hands and stopping every couple of feet to kiss the points right off his ears
- Boxers or briefs (saw this question in a *Cosmo*; isn't it coolio?): briefs, definitely briefs!
- Orli rating (this is what I'll rank all the other hotties against—Orlando is a perfect 100, so the other hotties will get points on how well they stack up to him): 100 because he's abso-perfectly perfect!

What do you think? Do you like? I think it'll be fun. You can help me pick hotties, if you like (you know, a little something to take your mind off Brent being a poophead for not calling you).

Now that I've shown you that, I need a little advice. It's not for me, really; it's about Holly. She was really peeved at me yesterday when I went out with Ruaraidh alone. Holly doesn't get peeved often, so when she does I pay attention.

She came in while I was getting dressed for the date. Oh, OK, it wasn't exactly a *date* date, but it was a kind-of date, don't you think? Anyhoodles, Holly came in while I was trying to decide between embroidered jeans or chinos.

"What are you doing?" she asked, watching as I tried the red crocheted top against the chinos.

"Just getting ready for my drive with Ruaraidh. Done with your sheep stuff for the day?"

"Yes, Alec said I was so good with the sheep, he'd let me work here during the summers if Mum said I could."

"V. cool!" I held the top up to me. "What do you think, is the red too much with the pink tee?"

She scrunched up her nose. "It makes my eyes water."

"Does it? Well, OK, how about with the apricot tee?"

"Better." She gnawed on her lip for a few minutes while I got changed. "I think you're being very selfish."

I peered at her as I pulled the apricot T-shirt with the tiny sparkly things in it over my head. "Huh? Selfish? *Me?* I share everything with you! I even let you borrow my ruffly purple gypsy skirt, and you know how much I love that!"

"You're not sharing Ruaraidh; you're keeping him all to yourself. I don't think it's fair for you to go off driving with him, and not let me come with you."

I made a little moue and went to the dressing table to check my makeup. "Holly, this is a competition, remember? Besides, Ruaraidh asked *me*, not you."

OK, now here's where it gets bad. I could see Holly in the mirror, and as soon as I pointed out to her that Ruaraidh asked me to do the driving thing, she bit her lip and turned away with a really hurt look on her face. Then she hugged Julian the teddy bear.

That made me feel awful! There I was all happy and everything, and Holly was just . . . well, *Holly*. Not geeky or anything, just a bit shy and young and stuff. Still, she was my friend, and because of that, I owed it to her to make her feel better. You know me, always thinking of others. "Um . . . Hol? That came out wrong. I'm sure if you were old enough to drive, and had your license, and were a visiting American who didn't know how to drive on the left, Ruaraidh would have asked you, too."

She shrugged her shoulders and picked at Julian's head.

I could see she didn't want me to talk about it, so I redid my makeup, spritzed some perfume in the air and walked through it (for that total-coverage impact that's so classy), then pulled on my wedge boots and jacket, and told her I'd see her later.

"Em?"

I paused at the door. "Yeah?"

"Do you . . . I know we're doing this competition and all, but do you think that Ruaraidh . . . likes me?"

Uh-oh.

"Of course he likes you; he likes you a lot. He smiles at you, and he talks to you when you guys are doing the sheep stuff, right?"

"Yes, but—"

"And he liked the cookies you made yesterday. A guy who doesn't like a girl won't tell her she makes great cookies, so that proves he likes you."

"That's not what I—"

"And he laughed at your joke about the sheep. You know the 'you and your ewe' joke. He wouldn't do that unless he liked you. It's a scientific fact that guys can't laugh at a joke unless they like the girl who told it."

"I'm not sure about that . . . but that's not what I meant, anyway. I meant, do you think he really likes me . . . in a girlfriendy sort of way? Could he, you know, ever be in love with me?"

Criminy dutch, why is it people always ask the "write an essay answer no less than three double-spaced pages" questions just before you're going out the door on an almost-date with a Schottie?

"Do you want him to be in love with you? Are you really serious about him?"

She nodded, and hugged Julian tighter. "I think he's wonderful. I think about him all day. I dream about him at night. I keep imagining what he'll say to me, and what I'll say to him, and what he's like when he kisses. He's the absolute best guy I've ever known!"

"Holly, I . . . uh . . . I'm sure he . . . um . . . oh, shoot, I'm late. I'll talk to you later about this,'kay?"

She did the shrug thing again, and put her headphones on, but I could tell later, when I came back, that she'd been crying. I tried to talk to her, but she wouldn't.

So what do you think I should I do? Should I end the competition and let her have him all to herself? I don't want to do that! I like Ruaraidh, too! I don't think he's the absolute best guy in the whole wide world, but I like him. A lot. And he likes me; he told me he likes me, so that's definitely a good thing, even if I did end up breaking his toe.

I just hate this! Why can't anything ever work out nice for me? Now Holly's going to make me feel horrible when Ruaraidh chooses me over her, and then she won't be my friend anymore, and I'll feel even worse because she doesn't have a lot of friends.

Why do I have to choose between them? Why???

Kissy hugs,
~Em

Subject: Oh, BTW . . .
From: Mrs.Legolas@kiltnet.com
To: Dru@seattlegrrl.com
Date: 8 January 2004 4:08pm

I forgot to tell you—the sweater is turning out really odd. The knitting book doesn't say anything about it having bumps and stuff in it, but mine does. And that's just the front side! Holly and I knit at night, when we watch TV. She's already done the front and back, and is getting ready to start on the sleeves. She doesn't have to look at her hands when she knits, but I do.

The problem is, when I watch myself knit, I forget how I'm supposed to do it, because it's confusing about whether you're supposed to put the yarn around the front of the knitting needle or the back. I've been switching back and forth to see which way I like best. I can't really tell a difference, to be honest, although Holly said it makes a big difference.

I think she was just showing off her knitting brilliance in front of Ruaraidh. I'm not too worried. Even lumpy, my sweater is going to be fabu! I think. I hope.

Sigh. Tell me again why I'm doing this?

Hugsies and kisses,
~Em

Subject: re: He called!!!!!!!!!!!!!!
From: Mrs.Legolas@kiltnet.com
To: Dru@seattlegrrl.com
Date: 9 January 2004 11:08am

Dru wrote:
> we talked for almost a whole hour! And he asked if he
> could take some black-and-white pics of me (b&w be-
> cause it's winter and everything looks starker in b&w—
> isn't he cool?), and of course I said yes! So we're going to
> Volunteer Park next weekend and he's going to take pics!

I told you he likes you, didn't I? I *told* you! I just knew he
had to be serious, because film and stuff costs money, and
since he doesn't have a job or anything, you have to know
that if money doesn't matter to him, he's madly in love with
you.

Tell me everything that happens tomorrow! And send me
scans of the pics when you get to see them.

> Back to you . . . you ran over his foot?

It was an accident! I didn't mean to!

> You *ran over* his foot?

Just a little bit. Hardly at all. In fact, if the doctor hadn't
told him his toe was broken in two places, I doubt if he
would have noticed it.

> As for the situation with Holly, all I can says is, Ugh! Is
> this her first crush? If it is, you've got; problems, GF. You

> remember how you felt about your first crush—you
> swore you were going die if Peter didn't take you to the
> Sophomore Harvest Dance, and he didn't, but you didn't
> die. I still have that voodoo doll you made of him, you
> know. I can't believe you sewed a little thingy on it, and
> then poked a bunch of pins in it before hacking it off with
> a knife.

Oh! Thank you for reminding me, I want to make one of Aidan, and I forgot I'd left Voodoo Peter with you. Could you pop it in the mail for me? I'll just change its hair and sew on its arms and legs and thingy, and it'll do for Aidan.

Re: Holly—yes and no. She had a bit of a pash on a guy last year, but it didn't pan out. He was much older than her and didn't pay her any attention. I think that's probably why she's so uptight about Ruaraidh thinking she's too young.

I'm going to try to talk to her and see if she's really in love with him, or just *thinks* she is. You know how sometimes guys can fool you that way.

Gotta run. Alec is coming up to look at the database after lunch, which means I'd better stop playing with the Hottie of the Week page and start getting some of the sheep data entered.

Hugs and sheepy kisses,
~Em

Subject: re: Burns Night
From: Mrs.Legolas@kiltnet.com
To: DevTheMan@britnet.co.uk
Date: 10 January 2004 9: 11am

DevTheMan wrote:
> Fang is going to drive up with me, so that's cool. I don't
> mind sleeping on the couch. As long as you are there,
> that's all I care about. The circus in Inverness sounds fun.
> We should roll up sometime around lunch on Sunday, if
> that's OK.

Yay! I'm so glad you and Fang are coming; it's going to be a blast going to Inverness with you guys! The circus isn't really a circus; it's more like a carnival, with rides and palm reading and a sideshow and stuff like that. I know it's kind of silly and juvie-sounding, but Holly really wants to go and have her palm read. Maybe we could do a club or something after?

Ruaraidh may come with us. I asked him, but he's not sure if he wants to (he's the guy who's working for Alec). I accidentally ran over his foot the other day, but it's OK; he just broke one toe. He's almost stopped limping now.

Oh, hey, do you still have that dreamy picture of you in your knight costume? Can I have a copy? I'd like you to be on my Hottie of the Week site. I could put up that picture of you as a knight. I bet it'll get a lot of attention!

Oh! Guess what? Holly and Aunt Tim and I are going to another castle tomorrow. It's supposed to be a really great castle, not just ruins, so I'm chuffed. The last one we went to was a disaster (a bunch of broken castle, and I hurt my knees), but this one is supposed to be really famous, and was used in a bunch of movies and stuff.

How is the semester going for you? Did you get into that structural engineering class you wanted? Tell me what's going on with you—I miss you guys terribly!

Hugs and squeezes,
Emily

Subject: OH MY CROD!
From: Mrs.Legolas@kiltnet.com
To: Dru@seattlegrrl.com
Date: 11 January 2004 8:01pm

That's it, I'm not interested in castles *anymore!* They can all fall down and turn to mush for all I care. If I *ever* have to live through another experience like the one I lived through today, I'm going to become a nun and live in a nunnery and never see anyone ever again.

Meh!

I do have to say, the paramedics in Scotland are really cute.

Yeah, yeah, I'm getting to it; just let me tell it in my own way, OK?

This morning Aunt Tim took Holly and me to Nethercote Castle, which is about an hour and half away. Alec and Ruaraidh didn't come. Alec said he'd had enough culture to last him the rest of the year, and Ruaraidh said—with a particularly unfair look at me—that his foot hurt and he didn't want to walk around a lot. Which is just silly, because he walks around all day out with the sheep; how could walking around a civilized castle hurt any more than walking in sheep poop?

Anyhoo, we drove out to the castle, singing along to Aunt

Tim's Beatles CD, which was v. fun (I thought about having a thing for Paul McCartney, but then I saw a picture of him now, and he's *old*!). This castle is set on a little island, with a long, curved gray stone bridge that you walk over to get into the castle. It's really big, too! Not the bridge, silly, the castle.

"All right, girls, we'll show those men we don't need them along to have fun in a castle, right?"

"Um," I said. "Well, actually—"

"Right," Aunt Tim said firmly, then pulled out Brother's castle book as we walked through a big stone doorway at the end of the bridge. "Let's see, this would be the famed Nethercote portcullis. This says there's an inscription above the portcullis that we shouldn't miss seeing."

We looked.

"This is *so* not exciting," I said. "It's just, like, words! When do we get to the good part of the castle?"

"Yes, well, I must admit I don't see the *must-see* aspect of the inscription," Aunt Tim said, pushing Holly forward. "But we've seen it; now we can move on."

"I thought it was interesting," Holly protested.

"You're going to be a vet, remember?" I whispered, and pinched her. "You can't like history stuff if you're going to be a vet."

"I can, too! I can like whatever I want to like."

Aunt Tim stopped on the other side of the archway. "And this must be the famed Nethercote courtyard."

I suppose as courtyards go, it was OK. There wasn't much to see other than stone buildings, grass, and black railings to keep people out of certain areas. "Thrillsville. Where're the suits of armor, and the piper, and the pictures of knights in their really cool medieval-knight wear?"

Aunt Tim flipped through the book. "I'm not sure there are pictures of knights in Nethercote, Emily. There's a map here . . . hmmm. Well, there's a dungeon."

"Ooooh! Dungeons?" Holly asked.

I was right with her. Dungeons! "Coolio! We like dungeons! Does it have skeletons and stuff? I want my picture taken with a skeleton!"

"Maybe it has a rack and an iron maiden," Holly said, her eyes all bright and shiny like they get when she goes on about historical stuff.

"I'll take the rack; you take the iron maiden," I said. She giggled.

"I'm sorry, girls; the book says the dungeon sustained significant damage by flooding in 1999, and has been closed for repairs since then."

"Well, sheesh, that's like a million years ago. It must be working by now."

"Hmm. I'll ask. Now"—Aunt Tim waved toward a door to one of the buildings—"here we have the famed—"

"Good morning! Welcome to Nethercote." A short, frumpy-looking woman wearing a blue blazer with the words *Tour Guide* embroidered over her right boob marched over to us. "You wish to see the castle? Excellent. I will be happy to show you the rooms open to the public."

"That's very kind of you, but we have this book—" Aunt Tim started to say, but Edna (her name was embroidered over her left boob—either that, or she'd named her boobs! Hee!) shook her head and swung open a heavy wooden door.

"Visitors are not allowed to roam freely inside the castle."

"But—" Aunt Tim said.

"The grounds outside are open to the public, but inside

all visitors must be accompanied by a guide. We have had significant incidences of vandalism in the last few years, you understand. All visitors must now be escorted through the rooms."

"But we—"

"If you will come this way, we will proceed to the billeting room."

"But—"

"The walls of the billeting room are fourteen feet thick. You will notice the unique barrel-vaulted ceiling, which is two and a half feet thick."

"But—" I said, just to help Aunt Tim out. Edna spun around and flared her nostrils at me (why do old people do that? It's so grotty!).

"Yes? You have a question?"

"Um . . . yeah, sure. Can we see the dungeon?"

"The dungeon is closed for repairs. In here, you will see many exhibits concerning life at Nethercote, including a wool-winding wheel, a Sheraton writing bureau, and a Chippendale gaming table."

"Can we just peek into the dungeon?" I asked as Edna herded us forward into a room. I don't know what she was so excited about; it was just a room with a low curved ceiling and a bunch of stuff. You know, room stuff—chairs, tables, that sort of thing. There certainly wasn't anything coolio like a skeleton or torture rack. Not even a suit of armor.

"No, the dungeon is off-limits to visitors. Workmen are reinforcing the walls and floor; until they are finished, it is too dangerous to visit." She turned back to the room and waved at one of the walls that had a bunch of paintings on it. Aunt Tim and Holly went to look where she pointed. "Over there you will find several interesting pictures depicting various aspects of the history of Nethercote, as well as two authentic cannonballs found during recent renovations."

I put my hands on my hips. "What if I just stood in the doorway of the dungeon and looked in?"

"No," Edna said, her lips thinning.

"Look, I'm an American. I'm a visitor to this country. I really want to see a real dungeon in a real castle, and Urquhart didn't have one."

"No!" Edna said, a lot louder and meaner. She turned her back to me and started telling Aunt T and Holly about some guy who used to live at the castle.

"My dad is a medieval professor, for your information. He knows all sorts of stuff about castles and things, and I just bet you he'd want me to see the dungeon."

"The dungeon is off-limits," Edna said, her teeth doing a little grinding thing.

"Yeah, but I—"

"*I said no!*" Edna bellowed, then shot me a horrible look when another tour guide (her left boob was named Beverly) came in with a group of tourists. Edna took a long, deep breath, then made a hissing noise as she let it out. Just like a snake or something! Creepy, huh? Obviously she was insane.

"If you have all seen enough, we will move on to the banqueting hall. This way, please."

I thought about telling Edna that I'd do just about anything to see the dungeon, but Aunt Tim gave me one of her patented old-people "don't embarrass me" looks, so I decided I'd just take matters into my own hands.

We climbed a stone staircase to the next floor, which was basically one big room. There were banners and pictures and coats of arms and little Xs of crossed knives on the wall.

"Well, this is a little better," I said, wandering down the long room. "Weapons, cool!"

"Do not touch the weapons, please. As you can see, the banqueting hall is known for its grandeur. Within this room are fine examples of Sheraton—"

"Hey, Holly, look! A sword just like yours!"

"—and Chippendale furniture. *Please do not touch the weapons!*"

"Keep your hair on; we're not touching it."

"Emily," Aunt Tim said warningly.

I smiled at Edna.

She gave me a look like she'd like to see me gutted on the sword, then turned back to the room and waved her hand all around at things, blathering on about furniture and pictures and other dull stuff.

"You will notice the large circular wrought-iron chandelier hanging from the oak-timbered ceiling," Edna said, smiling up at the chandelier like it was her best friend.

"Emily! Look! A suit of armor!" Holly was down at the other end of the room, near a little recessed area.

"No! Really? Where? Fabu! Hey, Edna, tell us about the suit of armor!"

She sighed a sigh just like Brother does when he says I'm driving him to an early grave, but toddled down to where Holly stood admiring a suit of armor. It was pretty, I'll say that, although it looked awfully small. It was about my size, shorter than Aunt Tim. I thought those knight guys were bigger than that?

"This suit of armor dates back to the fifteenth century, and was acquired during one of the many battles between

the Scots and the English. As you can see, it has been—
Please do not touch it!"

I rolled my eyes at Holly, and pulled back my hand. "I
wasn't going to hurt it. I just want to see what the metal
feels like."

"The objects in Nethercote are all very valuable and frag-
ile. Visitors are asked not to touch *anything*."

She gave me a good glare, then went on to tell about the
English knight who had been killed, then went over to a
case that had some famous punch bowl or something. I
don't know; I wasn't paying much attention because my
fingers were practically itching to touch that suit of armor.
You know how it is when you want something so bad you
can almost taste it—I had to touch it. Just once, just a little
touch, but I had to know what it felt like.

I know, you're thinking: a suit of armor? But honestly,
Dru, it was really almost pretty, not rusty and ugly like you'd
expect, but glossy and shiny. I couldn't help it; I just *had* to
touch it.

I waited until Aunt Tim was bent over the case looking at
something, then told Holly to stand in front of me so Edna
wouldn't see.

Holly looked shocked, and grabbed my arm as I reached
toward the shiny metal front piece. "You're not going
to . . . Emily, she said you weren't supposed to!"

"Don't be silly; I'm not going to hurt it! I just want to feel
it. It looks all cold and slicky and very, very cool. Besides, I
can't go back home and tell all my friends that I saw a suit
of armor but couldn't touch it just because a woman whose
left boob is named Edna said not to! I *do* have my reputation
to think of!"

"Reputation?"

"Yeah. Hang on; she's looking over this way. Act like we're talking about the suit of armor."

"We *are* talking about the suit of armor."

I turned around to glare at her, my hands on my hips just like Mom does when she gets peeved at Brother. "What are you, a baby?"

Her eyes opened up wide. "No, of course I'm not a baby!"

"Yeah? Well, you're acting like one!"

"I don't think acting in a responsible manner—"

I poked her in the arm. "You're not acting in a responsible manner; you're acting scared."

She got all huffy over that. "I am not scared!"

"Yes, you are; you're scared that Edna will get mad at you. Crod, Holly, I don't see how you can expect that someone as slobbericious as Ruaraidh could like a girl who was scared of someone named Edna!"

"I'm not scared," she repeated. "I just don't happen to think it's a good idea to touch the suit of armor."

"Oh, get real. Do you honestly think I'm going to hurt it?"

She chewed on her lower lip. "Well, no . . ."

"Good, because I'm not. I just want to run my fingers over it. How can that hurt it?"

She chewed her lip a bit more. "I suppose it can't, not if you're careful."

"I'm always careful." I peered over her shoulder. "OK, she's looking the other way. Ooooh, it's cold. But very cool. I wonder if they waxed it? It's so shiny. Huh, doesn't feel very heavy. I wonder if I could—"

I swear, the *clatter*, *clang*, and *whumpa-whumpa ker-THUD* of the suit of armor's right arm as it fell off the shoulder and banged into the stone wall before crashing into the floor could be heard for miles.

Holly moaned and closed her eyes. I picked up the arm and hurriedly tried to reattach it before Edna noticed, but before I could, Edna ran over to me, snatched it out of my hand (scraping my knuckle when she did, the big bully), and shook it in front of my face. "I told you not to touch it. Did I not tell you? I did, I told you. *Now* look what you've done!"

"Ooops! Sorry. I barely touched it," I said, trying to work up a pout, but it wouldn't come. You know how it is with pouts . . . when you know you're in the wrong, the pout just won't happen. "Is it . . . um . . . broken? 'Cause I didn't mean to hurt it, honest. I just wanted to feel it. It's so slicky and cold and metalish. Aunt Tim, you should really feel this; it's very cool—"

Edna rehung the arm on the wooden frame holding up the suit of armor (it wasn't hurt at all, BTW), then turned to grab my arm (hard!) and shoved me out of the room. "Visitors are not to touch *anything in the castle*. Do I make myself understood? *Not one single, solitary thing!*"

"Well, duh. You're yelling it in my ear. I'm not an imbecile, you know."

She muttered something that I figured was pretty rude, then dragged us off to the next building to see another room. We saw the kitchens (dirty) and buttery (butterish—ha! That's a joke), and a bunch of other stuff. Every time I went to look at something, she was right there next to me, watching me with black, mean little eyes.

It wasn't until we saw the main hall that she let up on me, and that's probably because there was nothing there but a bunch of banners hanging from the ceiling.

There was also a small sign next to a dark staircase that said, *Dungeon*.

Sigh. I know, I know, I didn't do a very good job of telling this, did I? 'Cause I'm willing to bet you know exactly what happened next. Well, maybe not *exactly*, but the basic idea, which is, of course, that I went to see the dungeon.

We had to exit the main hall because Edna was too suspicious to leave us alone there. Aunt Tim wanted to go down to see some war monument or something. "Do you girls want to come with me, or shall we meet back at the car in fifteen minutes?"

"Oh, let's meet back at the car," I said quickly, pinching Holly's wrist so she wouldn't say anything. "We'll just wander around outside here and look at the windows and stuff."

Aunt Tim gave me another one of those ancient-relative looks. "You're not planning on touching anything, are you?"

I put my hands behind my back. "Nope, not a thing! We'll just look at stuff."

"Well . . . all right. Fifteen minutes."

"Oh, don't give me that look," I said to Holly when Aunt Tim left. "I wasn't lying! I meant what I said; I won't touch anything."

"Oh, good," she said, sighing in relief.

"I won't have to, because you're going to do it for me. Come on, the coast is clear; open the door for me."

"What?" she shrieked. I clapped a hand over her mouth and looked around quickly to make sure no one had heard her. We were standing just outside of the main hall in a sheltered corner. Because of the flood damage, there wasn't much to see in the main hall, so not many people came over to this area.

"Shhh! You have to open the door; I promised I wouldn't touch anything. And I mean it; we're just going to have a really quick peek at the dungeon."

"Emily—"

"What are you, a rabbit or a girl who is worthy of the love of an extremely hunkitudinous guy?"

She opened and closed her mouth a couple of times, then grabbed the door and yanked it open, growling, "I *hate* it when you do that!"

"Yeah, I know, but I really do have your best interests at heart. Brother says you have to have backbone if you're going to get anywhere in this cutthroat world, and a quick peek at a dungeon is just the thing to give you backbone. Come on, the hall is empty."

Holly hung back by the door. I dragged her forward. "I promise I won't touch anything!"

"You swear?"

"I absotively swear I won't touch one single atom in this building."

"Well, all right, but we have to be quick. And if you touch anything, Emily Williams, I'll never forgive you!"

We dashed across the hall quick like bunnies, crawled under the black velvet rope across the entrance to the stairs, then raced down the dark stairs to the dungeon.

Now, here's the thing—you know how Edna the Hun said that the dungeon was being worked on? Well, evidently she was telling the truth. What I found out later is that they'd piled up a bunch of stuff from the water-damaged part of the dungeon onto the stairs. Because the area was not open to the public, the lights weren't on, so I couldn't exactly see where I was going. I could see a little bit because there was light coming from the main hall, but not a whole lot, just enough to see that there was stuff piled on one side of the curvy stone steps.

Stuff like boxes, and piles of stone, and bits of metal, and some pieces of a table, and wood . . . and, as it turns out, a big metal thing at the bottom. It's called a mantrap, and it's like the things you see in the movies where a guy is out walking in the woods, and he steps on something, and big jaws spring shut and lock on his leg. This mantrap didn't have spiky claw bits like some do, but it still could spring shut. Hard!

Yes, you guessed it, on my leg.

"*Ack!*" I screamed when I stepped down onto the bottom step. Something (I didn't know then what it was) slammed onto my ankle and held it tight. "OHMICROD, one of the castle's ghosts has got me! *Ack!* Holly, help! Get whatever this is off of me! It hurts!"

"You touched something!" She bumped into me as she tried to pass me on the narrow stairs. "You promised me you wouldn't!"

"I didn't touch it; it touched me! Just help me and save the lecture for later."

We were at the bottom of the stairs, in the blackest part of the staircase, the light coming from the top of the stairs too weak for me to see what I was standing in. Holly felt her way down my leg, then rustled around my feet.

"It feels metal. It feels like a . . . like a trap."

"A trap?"

"The kind they use on wild animals. I can't . . . ergh . . . I can't open it."

I felt my way down the wall to my foot. "Here, let me

95

help. Maybe if you take one side and I take the other . . . Ow! I broke a nail!"

Even in the darkness I could hear Holly sigh. "If you hadn't touched anything—"

"I didn't touch anything! Poop! I can't see anything here; I'm going to have to go up to the light. Let me . . . ow! . . . see if I can . . . *ow* . . . make it up the . . . *ow!* . . . damned stairs."

The trap had a long chain attached to it, which was tangled up in the spokes of a wooden round thing (I have no idea what it was, but I just bet you it was a torture device), which made it hard to move. Of course, it didn't help having this huge metal thing clamped down on my ankle.

I clanked and thumped and swore my way up the stairs (Holly was shocked by the swearing. You know me, I'm not a potty-mouth, but there are times when you just have to let good taste go and give in to your inner bad girl). By the time we made it to the top of the stairs at the still-empty hall, I was panting and fighting back tears (the trap *hurt*!), and Holly looked like she was going to barf.

"Don't you dare ralph," I said, shaking my finger at her. "If you do, I will too, and I'm having a bad enough day without throwing up all over. Can you pull this thing off me?"

She squatted down and tried to pry the jaws open, but it wasn't giving. "I think it's rusted shut or something," she said, her eyes going all swimmy.

"Oh, don't do that either," I said, my eyes doing the same thing. "I don't want to cry. I just want to get this off."

"Maybe your aunt can help?"

"I don't see how; she doesn't carry medieval-trap tools around with her. Oh, Crod! This castle totally blows!"

"I can go find Edna," Holly said, wiping back a few tears. "She's likely to know how to get it off."

"She's probably the one who set it there in the first place."

"She'll yell at you, too," Holly said, then looked thoughtful for a few minutes while I tried to pry the jaws open. "I think we need to get you back to the car. Then we can tell your aunt, and she'll take us home, and your uncle can use his tools to get it off."

I looked at her for a second, then down to the huge metal monstrosity hanging off my foot. "Holly, this thing weighs a gazillion pounds!"

"I'll help you walk," she said, putting her arm around me. "We'll do it slowly, so you won't stumble or fall."

"You're nutso-cuckoo! I can't go walking out of here with this thing! People will see me!"

She sucked her lip for a second, then pulled her coat off. "I'll wrap my coat around your foot, and people will think . . ."

"Yes?" I asked as she squatted at my feet, her coat in her hands. "Just what will they think? That I'm some sort of weirdo coat perv who likes to wear coats on her foot?"

"I'm just trying to help," she snapped. "If you hadn't touched—"

"Oh, Crod!" I yelled, so frustrated I could just spit. And you know I *never* spit!

In the end Holly went to find my aunt Tim while I hid on the stairs in case anyone came in to look at the empty main hall. Aunt T took one look at my foot and went to find Edna, who did exactly what you think she did—lectured me up one side and down the other; then she called the fire department because it turns out the stuff that was on the stairs was damaged by the water and there wasn't a key or whatever it is you use to open up a moldy old mantrap.

I had to sit outside on a stone while the paramedic guys looked at my foot, and all the tourists there stopped to watch, so by the time one of the firemen got a saw out to saw the trap off me, there were millions of people staring at Emily the Idiot, the only person in the last couple of hundred years to be caught in a mantrap.

So help me Crod, I am never going to another castle again in my whole entire life!

Hugs and kisses,
~Em

Subject: re: Get your Goth name site
From: Mrs.Legolas@kiltnet.com
To: Fbaxter@oxfordshire.agricoll.co.uk
Date: 11 January 2004 10:40pm

Fbaxter wrote:
>> Fang, you have to go to this really cool site! You type
>> in your name and it gives you your Goth name! Mine
>> is Dread Queen. Isn't that coolio? I'm *so* Dread Queen!
>
> Mine is Addicted Sex Slave. Not sure whether I should
> be pleased or not.

I think it's . . . um . . . OK, it's not very good. Did you do Francis instead of Fang? 'Cause if you do Fang Baxter you get Tortured Midnight.

Guess that isn't very much better, is it?

Holly's name is Weeps Silent Terror, which is v. cool, although I don't think it really fits her. See you and Devon in two weeks! I can't wait—I miss you guys so much!

Smoochies,
Emily

Subject: re: You did WHAT in a castle?
From: Mrs.Legolas@kiltnet.com
To: Hwilliams@mediev-l.oxford.co.uk
Date: 12 January 2004 10:10am

Hwilliams wrote:
> Timandra says you had an adventure recently in a castle.
> She wouldn't say how it happened (although long ac-
> quaintance with you leaves me in little doubt it was
> something you did), but that you ended up locked into a
> mantrap. She also says you sustained nothing worse than
> bruises. Since I am only the man who fathered you, the
> man who spends everything he has to support you, I don't
> suppose you would care to tell me the exact sequence of
> events that led to your being locked into a mantrap?

Um . . . no, not really.
So, how are things there at Ye Olde Haunted Mansion? Any ghosts or assorted other creepy things pop up in that weird house you insist we live in?

I'm doing fine here. Alec gave me an *excellent* on my first week's evaluation, and said I was a genius at the computer. He really liked the database I set up, although he had me add in some fields for gross things like fertility info (like I want to sit here and type up when all the sheep get their periods?), and which sheeps' babies died, and which ones were sent off to make lamb chops, and other icky stuff.

I'm starting to see the attraction of being a vegetarian.

Holly also got an *excellent*, although she didn't get the genius comment about sheep (but he did say she had a natural empathy for livestock, which I suppose is good). Next weekend we're going to Aberdeen for an official kilt watch, and to see some Scottish dancing, which Aunt Tim says is really cool because there're lots of guys who go to see the girls, and swords and stuff. V. educational, don't you think? Don't you think that such a good learning experience should be encouraged? I thought you would. £25 should make me appreciate all the fine educationalishness of the trip. If you send it today, I'll have it by Saturday.

Ta!
Emily

Subject: HOTW is up!
From: Mrs.Legolas@kiltnet.com
To: Dru@seattlegrrl.com
Date: 12 January 2004 3:50pm

Just wanted to let you know that I got the first official Emily's Hottie of the Week up early today. I posted the URL on a couple of sites, and already I'm getting feedback! Of course, everyone loves Orlando except some complete loser who thinks Elijah Wood is cuter—excuse me? Cute, yes, but cuter? Fwah!

Next week's HOTW is going to be Devon. Yeah, yeah, I

know he's not a famous star, but he is *so* snogworthy, and he sent me the picture of him in his knight's costume (the one he wore to the Vampire Ball), and I'm telling you, it just makes my knees go all funny when I look at it. Anyhoo, I'm making him HOTW #2, which will go up next Monday.

Let me know when you're back from your skiing weekend. And be sure to tell me if any hotties fell for your snow-bunny routine!

Hugs and kisses,
~Em

Subject: re: What if he thinks I'm hideous? Wah!
From: Mrs.Legolas@kiltnet.com
To: Dru@seattlegrrl.com
Date: 14 January 2004 7:11pm

Dru wrote:
> until Sunday. What do you think I should wear for the
> pictures? What will look good in black and white? What
> if the pictures turn out awful?!? He'll never want to see
> me again. You don't think he just wants to take my pic-
> ture because I'm, like, a freak or something? *Ack!*

We need to work on your self-image, Dru; we really do. *Of course* he doesn't want to take your picture because you're a freak! He likes you! He's just using the pictures as an excuse to see you! Sheesh, didn't you learn anything from that "What Guys Say and What They Really Mean" article I showed you last year? Guys never come right out and say that they think you're hot (unless they're like

Devon—really flirty). Instead they do things to hang out with you. So stop worrying already! Re: what to wear—definitely the bomber jacket and the skirt you got for Christmas.

I had to go out and help with the sheep today. I'm beginning to think the sheep have cursed me or something. I mean, there's just no other explanation for the things that happen when Alec drags me out into the mud and poop.

"Emily, I'll be needin' you to lend a hand out in the fields today," Alec said at breakfast, which was a cue for the ominous sheep-attack music to start.

"I thought you said I wasn't allowed to go near them after the last time, when I accidentally left the gate open and all the withers ran out, and it took you two days to get them back?"

Alec stabbed his fork into a piece of ham. Really hard, like he was trying to kill something. "They were wethers, lass, and aye, I did, but even you can't muck this up."

I thought about getting all shirty about that muck-up comment (*shirty* means *pissed*), but decided that since Alec had given me a good report for the first week—and hadn't mentioned any of my problems with the sheep—I would cut him a little slack. "What is it you want me to do?"

"The local vet and a couple of vet students will be out today scannin' the ewes, and I'll need you all to mark them once they've been scanned."

"Scanned?" Holly asked. "Do you put some sort of electronic tag in them?"

Ruaraidh came in just then. "Alec, the vet and his team just arrived."

Alec swore under his breath, and grabbed a piece of toast before he went outside.

"Scanning is when the vet does an ultrasound on the

ewes to see how many lambs she's carrying," Aunt Tim said. "You know how they do ultrasound scans on pregnant women?"

Holly blushed and stared down at her plate. I watched Ruaraidh a bit worriedly as I nodded. Ever since the first day, when Brother made a scene about me having babies with Ruaraidh, he's been a bit weird whenever the subject comes up. Not that we sit around and talk about having babies or anything—you know I'm not going to have the first of my three children (Chloe, Annie, and Jack) until I've won the Nobel prize, which I figure will be when I'm twenty-four.

"The principle is the same with the ewes. The vet scans their bellies and tells us how many lambs they're carrying."

Holly poked at her breakfast while Ruaraidh scarfed down ham and scrambled eggs and—this is just so gross—beans on toast, and a grilled tomato. *For breakfast!*

I stuck to the toast, minus beans, and eggs.

"So why's the number of babies the sheep has so important?" I asked. "Can't you just wait until they pop out and then count them up?"

Ruaraidh looked up. "It's important to know because the ewes carrying twins and triplets need more food, for one."

"It also helps to know at lambing time," Aunt Tim added, then toddled off to get her boots.

"Oh. I guess that makes sense. So what are we supposed to do?"

Alec and the vet came in just then. "You done with your breakfast? Good. Ruaraidh, this is Tom Merritt, our vet. You'll be workin' with Tom on the south hill. Holly, lass, I'd like you to do Clown with Tom's assistant, Sarah."

OK, "Clown" isn't really the name of the hill, but it has

some weird Gaelic spelling, and I'm too pooped to look it up. It *sounds* like Clown.

"Emily . . ." Alec eyed me carefully, then sighed. "I'm short of hands or I wouldn't be havin' you out on the parks. You'll do the lowground ewes with Sarah. I've the bags with the paint outside. Don't be forgettin' to make notes in the notebook."

Alec turned and started back out the door, the short, bald vet named Tom right after him. Ruaraidh crammed an *entire* muffin in his mouth, and followed the two of them. I looked at Holly. She looked right back at me.

"Paint?" she asked.

"Notebook?"

She looked out the window as the three guys passed, heading for the gate into the nearest pasture. Two other people stood down by the barn, wearing thick coats and hats and mufflers and gloves, each one with a gray canvas bag slung over one shoulder. Aunt Tim joined Alec and the vet as they wandered over. "I guess we'd better go find out."

We got out there a couple of minutes later and were introduced to the vet students (I'll have to remember to ask Fang if he does ultrasounds). My vet partner was Sarah Starr (just a little taller than me, long blond braid, cute but with no fashion sense), who was really nice, if a bit of an airhead. She wasn't really ditzy, just a bit scared of doing ultrasounds on her own.

OK, she was clueless. But I didn't know that at first.

Ruaraidh gave Holly and me each a cloth bag that had three cans of spray paint and a little notebook. "What's the spray paint for?" I asked, checking the bag. There was black, blue, and red paint.

"We mark the ewes to know how many lambs they're carrying," Ruaraidh said. He was watching Sarah as she fussed with her black ultrasound box. I waved my hand in front of his face. His head snapped around to look back to Holly and me. "Oh, sorry. If the ewe has a single, you don't do anything; just make a note in the notebook. For twins, you make a blue mark. For triplets, red. For quads, black. Make a note of the ear tag number and the number of lambs. Got it?"

"Um . . ."

"Good. Sarah, tell me, how long have you been at the vet college?"

Ruaraidh walked off toward the pasture with Sarah. Holly and I looked at each other with *both* our mouths hanging open.

"He didn't just do that," I said. "Tell me he didn't just glom onto another girl when you and I were standing right here in front of him?"

"He did," Holly said, snapping her mouth closed. "He just . . . left."

She did that little throat thing you do when you want to cry but don't want anyone to see, then turned away and started off to the pasture. I grabbed both our bags and caught up to her.

"You know, if he's going to do things like this, I'm starting to think that maybe he's not worth having a competition over."

She twitched a shoulder and took the bag I handed her. "Maybe. I suppose it doesn't matter. I'm not going to win, anyway."

"Sure, you could!" I said, trying to think of reasons why Ruaraidh would want to date her over me. I hate it when

Holly looks all hurt and stomped on. "You're ahead right now, aren't you?"

"Only by ten points."

"Yeah, well, ten points is ten points. And you've almost got your sweater done, which will be worth mega bonus points."

She muttered something and kicked at a weed.

"What?"

"I said the points don't matter."

I tossed my bag of paint over the fence and climbed over the wooden gate. "They don't? Then what does?"

Holly jumped down off the gate and picked up her bag, her lips a bit pouty (and not sexy pouty—hers were pity-party pouty). "Ruaraidh matters."

Ugh. I hate this. I hate her being madly in love with him. And no, I don't mean I hate it because I want him all to myself; I'm not that selfish. Well, OK, I am, but I have to admit that ever since Aidan, I've been a bit more cautious when it comes to guys. Aidan was so *über*-fabu, and then he turned into a complete and utter poophead. Ruaraidh is kind of doing the same thing—he is so very hot, but at the same time he does things that tick me off. Just a little bit. But then he can be nice, like when he took me driving and told me he liked me and all.

Meh! I wish I understood guys! I wish they'd be either scrummy or dillweeds, but not a mixture of both! It's so confusing when they're *both*! And why can't I figure out which Ruaraidh is?

Anyhoodles, we caught up to Sarah and Ruaraidh and everyone else; then we all split up. Sarah and I went out to the farthest field. Alec has sheep that live on the four hills that surround his farm, as well as on the flat area, which he calls the lowground (he's Scottish. You'll just have to trust me that it explains a whole lot).

Sarah was pretty cool, other than forgetting how to turn on the ultrasound machine that she carried in her backpack. Since I'm so *über*-hip when it comes to electronic stuff, I looked it over and found the on/off switch, and after that, things went well.

For a bit, anyway. OK, for about five minutes, until we did the first sheep.

The ultrasound machine had two parts—a black square console with a tiny screen, and a handheld thingy on a cord. Sarah would sneak up on a sheep, then move the handheld part around on the sheep's tummy. The babies were supposed to show up on the screen, although she showed it to me, and I never once saw anything that didn't look like a blotch. I couldn't see how she could tell between common ordinary sheep guts and babies, but evidently she could.

"This one . . . looks like this one has twins," Sarah said as she squatted in the muck next to a sheep. I was holding its neck so it wouldn't run off. "Yes, those are definitely twins."

"OK," I said, and grabbed the red can of paint. I sprayed a big number two on the sheep's side, then decided that I'd better do both sides, because if the sheep was standing one way, showing the side without the mark, Alec might think she just had one baby.

"Erm . . . my mistake. This one has just a single."

I gave Sarah a pissed-off look. "What do you mean, *your mistake*? I just wrote twos on her!"

"Sorry, I'm a bit new to this. I've only done sheep in the lab, you know. We flip them over on a cradle, and . . . well, it's much easier to read them like that. Here they're standing around and moving."

I tried wiping off the paint, but it just smeared. "Great, now I have a painty hand! What am I supposed to do? I can't take the paint off."

Sarah was muttering at her ultrasound machine, giving it a little smack. She wasn't really paying attention to me at all. "Hmm? Oh, just cross it out."

I sighed and rolled my eyes, but no one except the sheep saw me, so it was really a wasted effort. I grabbed the black paint and scribbled out the twos on either side of the sheep, making a note in the book that this sheep had only one lamb, and it wasn't my fault if it was painted red and black. I couldn't help it if I got the airhead vet student.

"All right, I think it's working now. If you'll just hold her head again, Emily, I'll give it another try."

"What?" I yelled, which made the sheep jump and go running off. "What do you mean you're going to give it another try? You just told me the sheep was a oner! I scratched out the two!"

Sarah looked at the sheep and grimaced. "Sorry, I didn't hear you. Let's just catch her and see what she has inside. Maybe she has a single."

"Yeah? And what am I supposed to do if she doesn't?"

"We'll worry about that later. You go over there and head her off, and I'll go this way."

We cornered the sheep (Sarah had to throw her jacket on the sheep's head to stop her) and did another ultrasound on her while I hung on to the sheep's stinky neck.

"Let's see what we have here . . . um. . . . blast, it's acting up again; let me just . . ." Sarah shook the machine a couple of times, checked its batteries, and finally ended up smacking it on the ground several times. "Got it! Hold her still, Emily."

"How am I supposed to do that?" I asked, trying my best to keep her from moving, but it's hard when all you're holding on to is a bunch of woolly neck.

"Hold her nose."

"What?"

"Hold her nose. Pinch it between your fingers. Not hard enough to hurt her, but hard enough so she won't move. I need her standing still so I can get an accurate reading."

"*Ew!* I'm not holding her nose! I'll get sheep snot on me!"

Sarah made one of those exasperated *tsk* noises, which is really unfair when you consider she was the one holding us up.

"Then hold her jaw."

I looked down at the sheep. "I'm not putting my fingers anywhere near her mouth. She's a wild animal! She'll bite me!"

"She won't bite you."

I made slitty eyes at her. "Oh, right, like you're an expert at this? You couldn't even find the on/off switch!"

"Sheep don't have on/off switches, and I am an expert with them. Or more of an expert than you are. She won't bite. Just hold her muzzle and let me do the reading!"

At the extremely dangerous risk of losing any or all of my fingers, I held the sheep's muzzle (she didn't like it and blew snot out her nose at me, which just made me glad I stood my ground re: the nose-holding bit).

"Here we go; here's the image. Just a few more seconds . . . one, two . . . oh. Triplets, I'm afraid."

We both looked at the sheep's side. The big red two (I'd written it really big, so it could be seen from a long way off) was scribbled out with black.

"All right," I said, shaking up the can of green. "But you

have to explain to Alec what happened. I don't want him thinking I don't know how to count."

I had to make the number three extra thick so it could be seen over the black and red, but it still wasn't too clear.

I'm going to skip over the next three hours, because it was pretty bad and I don't want to make you laugh so hard you'll barf, like you did that time when we were seven and you stood on the deck of the ferry and spat chewed-up hot dog onto the cars below. You can just take it from me that by the time we stopped for lunch, Sarah and I had done only about half the sheep we were supposed to do.

We gathered up our stuff and made the thousand-mile walk back to the house, where we had to de-poop our boots and wash up before Aunt Tim let us into the house.

"How did it go?" Alec asked us as we dived into a Welsh rarebit (it's a cheese sauce that you pour over toast. Aunt Tim makes it with beer—it's really nummy).

Sarah glanced over to me. "Fine."

"Yeah, fine," I said, wondering what Alec was going to say when he saw the sheep.

"No problems, then?"

"We were a little slow getting started," Sarah answered, keeping her eyes on her rarebit. "But I think we've got the hang of it now."

I choked on my iced tea and almost spewed it through my nose.

Alec raised his eyebrows at me as I coughed and hacked up my spleen trying to get the iced tea out of my lungs, but didn't say anything else.

"You are such a fibber," I told Sarah an hour later as we walked back out to our field of sheep.

"It wasn't a fib; we are getting better," she said a bit

huffily. I grabbed her arm and stopped, pointing to the sheep in front of us. About half of them had various colors of numbers painted on them, big black scribble marks, and another number painted over that.

"Better? You think that's better? Crod, Sarah!"

"Crod?"

"Private joke. What am I going to tell Alec?"

She jerked her arm away from me and started off toward an unmarked sheep. "You're worrying about nothing; he probably won't even notice."

I looked back at the sheep. "Won't notice? It looks like those sheep have been graffitized; of course he's going to notice! I swear, that one looks like we were playing tic-tac-toe on it."

"Well, you shouldn't be so quick to paint the numbers on them."

"We have a ton more sheep to do! Alec said we had to be quick. *I'm* being quick. You're the slowpoke on this team."

"If you'd wait until I was sure of the lamb count—"

"I'd be an old lady."

I spent the rest of the afternoon wondering if my sheep-dog skills were good enough to get Lass to move all the graffitied sheep over to Ruaraidh's hill so he'd get the blame for them, but in the end it didn't matter. Just before tea Alec came to help us, since he and Aunt Tim had finished their sheep. Aunt Tim stood with her eyes opened really wide and her hand over her mouth. Alec stared at the sheep for a few seconds, then turned to look at me.

I pointed to Sarah. "It's her fault. She's a bad ultrasoun-der."

Sarah stood up from where she was kneeling next to a

sheep, and glared at me. "I am not; the machine is acting up. And these sheep are difficult to read when they move. . . ."

Alec looked at the sheep wandering around grazing. Aunt Tim covered her eyes.

"I think they look kind of nice," I said, trying to make the best of the situation. "V. colorful. They brighten up the landscape, don't you think?"

Alec closed his eyes. "Why am I seein' smiley faces on my ewes?"

"Oh, those were the ones that Sarah was really sure of. The others were kind of iffy, so I thought it would help you if we marked the ones she was positive about. That way you know that their number is accurate. I put the smiley on their butts so you could see it from either side. The blue smilies are the ones she's really, really certain of, and the red smilies are the ones that she's about seventy-five percent sure of, and the black smilies are the ones that she was feeling pretty good about, but wasn't willing to swear to it in a court of law. Right, Sarah?"

"Erm . . . the machine has been acting up—"

Alec didn't say anything; he just turned around and walked away. Aunt Tim looked at the sheep for a couple of seconds more, opened her mouth to say something, then shook her head and followed Alec.

Sarah moaned something about the machine being broken, but I had other things to worry about. What if Alec flunks me for this week? The evaluations during work experience are really important! It goes on my official record! What if he blames me because I got Sarah to work with?

Gah. I thought things were supposed to get easier when you got older.

Have to run; Holly wants to use the computer. Let me know what's going on in the nonsheepy side of the world.

Hs and Ks,
~Em

Subject: Blech
From: Mrs.Legolas@kiltnet.com
To: Dru@seattlegrrl.com
Date: 16 January 2004 4:32pm

Dru wrote:
> was cute and all, but how could I think about dating him
> if I have Brent? OK, I don't have Brent yet, but I might,
> and then I'd be two-timing him, and you know after
> Vance the weasel (you were so right about him) did that
> to me. I swore never to two-time anyone.

Well, I'm not going to say I told you so, but *I told you so!* And no, even if the guy at Whistler was coolio and everything, if you're thinking about becoming serious with Brent, it's not good for you to be flirting with someone else. On the other hand, what if things with Brent fall through? If you flirted with Hans the ski instructor, then at least you'd have him to fall back on.

Oh, poop, I don't know what you should do. My love life is such a mess right now, I don't think I should be giving you advice. You'll just end up like me, looking like . . . Well, I'll get to that in a mo.

> Oh! I meant to tell you, I'm getting my baby next week.
> Do you guys get babies in England? I can't decide what

> to name mine, whether it should be a boy or a girl. Becca
> and Rach asked if they could have twins (duh—like they
> *are* twins!), but Mrs. Darling said no, only one baby per
> person. Anyway, I'm kind of dreading the baby, because
> you know what a hard time I have waking up in the
> middle of the night. And a doll that pees all over the place
> is just gross.

I think we get sacks of flour instead of the dolls that you
guys get. At least, that's what Lalla said, but I can't believe
that. I mean, the whole thing behind the babies is to show
you what having one is really like, right? So how can carrying
around a bag of flour tell you what a baby is like? I mean,
it doesn't wet its diapers, it doesn't have a microchip that
makes it wake up in the middle of the night; it just sits there.
It's a *sack of flour!* Anyway, we don't get those until next
semester. I thought you were all copacetic with the name
Sahara?

So let me tell you about the horrible thing that's happened. Before you ask if it was like the castle thing, it wasn't.
This is all Sarah's fault; I'm totally innocent. Well, mostly.
OK, so I had something to do with it, but . . . meh. Let me
tell this properly or you'll end up all confused.

Sarah is the vet girl who was here on Wednesday and
yesterday while they scanned the sheep. I was supposed to
help today, but Alec found someone at a neighbor's farm
to take my place, which was fine because that meant I could
work on the HOTW page. Anyway, they got done just after
lunch, and Alec gave Holly the rest of the afternoon off, so
we went into town to do some shopping. There's not a lot
of shops here because the town isn't very big, but there is

a chemist's (drugstore,'member?) and a very cool pizza place that shows old silent movies, and a bunch of ucky old-people shops.

Back to Sarah. When we were all having lunch, everyone was sitting around the table yacking away about stuff. Nothing exciting. No one mentioned the colorful sheep, although Sarah did say she was glad she had a partner who wasn't so fast off the mark with the paint can.

Whatever.

Then Ruaraidh started talking to Sarah about what she does in her spare time. Right in front of Holly and me! He's never asked us that!

"I like to rock-climb when I can," she answered, stuffing a huge forkful of pasta salad into her piehole. "I'm hoping to start training for some of the serious climbs this summer."

"Rock climbing—I've always wanted to try that," Ruaraidh said, smiling his "Scottish god of love and hunky thighs" smile at her. He was looking particularly hot, too, in really tight jeans and a soft blue mohair sweater that I just wanted to run my fingers over (you know how I love mohair. Right? Remember? I love mohair!).

"I like rock climbing, too," Holly said, which was a big fat lie, because I happen to know for a fact that she's afraid of heights. I gave her a "what are you doing?" look, but she just gave me the "shut up" signal (she stomped on my toe).

Poor girl. She really has it bad for Ruaraidh. I don't know what to do about it, either. Which do you think is kinder— should I make him fall madly in love with me, so she'll get over him, or should I help her make him fall in love with her, which I don't think he'll do because evidently he's interested in blond, rock-climbing vet wanna-bes?

"It's great fun, isn't it?" Sarah said to Holly, then went

off into some strange rock-climbing talk about carabiners and cams and harnesses . . . in other words, gibberish. I ignored most of it.

"I didn't know there was anywhere to climb in Scotland," Aunt Tim said.

"Oh, yes, there are lots of places, particularly in the Highlands. Applecross is my favorite, although I like Torridon tolerably well. In the winter I do hill walks and wilderness walks. My favorite is up Munro. It's so beautiful up there."

I asked. Munro is a mountain.

"Sounds strenuous. It must keep you in great shape," Aunt Tim said.

Sarah nodded. "Oh, yes, it's very strenuous, but it's good for you!"

"You look great," Ruaraidh told her with another smile. "Very healthy, with that tan and all."

"Thanks, but the tan isn't due to climbing—I just got back from Majorca," she said, smiling back at him, then turned to Holly. "I hope to try ice climbing on Glen Avon in the Cairngorms next month. Have you ever climbed on ice?"

Holly made a squeaky sound that I knew meant she couldn't think of anything to say. I decided that as her BFF, I'd better help her out.

"My mom has a cousin who got skin cancer from all the tanning she did," I said. "It was awful; she had to have chunks of tumors and stuff cut out of her skin. Mom won't let us go to tanning salons now."

"Ew," Sarah said. "Nasty."

"Yeah, it was. My sister, Bess—she's really into healthy stuff like seaweed and sprouts and cultures and things—says girls who tan a lot look like they're eighty by the time they're thirty. Their skin gets all leathery and stuff."

All right, I know you know I don't believe it at all when Bess goes off on one of her health kicks, but hey, I never once said I believed it! I just said that's what my sister says. So I wasn't lying.

"I've never seen a girl with leathery skin." Ruaraidh laughed, his eyes crinkling up really cute. I waited for my insides to do the squidgy thing that they do when he eye-crinkles, but for some reason, I was squidgyless. "I like girls who are tanned. They look really healthy."

Holly and I did the eyebrow thing with each other (you know, the eyebrow thing. The talking-with-eyebrows thing). Holly raised her left eyebrow to say, *He likes tanned girls. Do you think he really just likes Sarah, and not all tanned girls?*

I scrunched up my right eyebrow, which said, *No, I think he means that he really likes girls who are muscley and tannish and healthy-looking.*

Then Holly lowered her right brow to say, *I'm not tan or muscley or healthy-looking.*

And I raised both of my eyebrows really high, then dropped them both down low, which meant, *You are too healthy-looking! You look über-fabu healthy! You have really nice hair, and no pimples, and you're not too skinny or too fat; you're just right. That's healthy! So stop feeling inferior to Vet Girl. You might be a bit pale, but we can fix that easily.*

Holly blinked, which as you know means she was asking, *How?*

I waggled my eyebrows up and down, which said, *We'll find the local tanning shop and get you tanned, girlfriend!*

Then Alec said, "What the devil are you two lasses doin'?"

and everyone at the table looked at Holly and me, which just made her blush.

"Eyebrow semaphore," Aunt Tim said as she sliced up an apple tart and handed it around.

"What?" Alec asked, staring at Holly and me like we were aliens or something. Sheesh! He might be a hottie older guy with a really delish accent, but he was utterly clueless!

"Eyebrow semaphore. All teens do it."

"They do?"

"I'll explain it to you later, sweetie."

Aunt Tim let me borrow her car after lunch, so after a huge, long lecture during which she made me swear that I a) would stay on the left and wouldn't speed, b) wouldn't go anywhere else but straight to town and back again, and c) wouldn't dance to the music on the radio while driving (what fun is listening to the radio if you can't seat dance?), I drove Holly to town. I hit only three things on the way there—just little hits, not big ones—and one of them wasn't my fault (the stop sign was in a stupid spot). Would you believe that they don't have a tanning salon here? I asked at the local hair place, but they said they haven't had one for years, which is just stupid. Who doesn't want a tan?

"What are we going to do?" Holly said, twisting the friendship bracelet I gave her for Christmas. "I don't stand a chance with Ruaraidh unless I'm tanned like Sarah."

I looked down the street. There wasn't much to see, just a few shops and offices and boring stuff. "Well, if we can't do this the authentic way, then I think we'll just have to do it artificially."

"Artificially? *We?*"

I grabbed my purse from the car and started toward the chemist. "Yes, we. You don't think I'm going to go around looking all fish-belly white next to you while you're Caribbean-goddess tan, do you? We'll get some sunless tanning lotion. I hate to use it. It's kind of a cheat and all, not nearly as good as a real tan, but there are times when you just have to lower your standards and make the best of a bad situation. Don't worry; we'll be gorgeous."

Her face got all scrunchy. "Oh. I didn't know you were going to do it, too."

She looked so hurt and made me feel so bad that I almost told her she could have Ruaraidh. I know, I never thought I'd even think about giving up an eleven-fingered Scottish god of love, but I've said all along that although he was majorly hunkalicious and all, I didn't want him to ruin our friendship.

But on the other hand, I should have just as much right to him as she has, right? I mean, that's only fair. And he *did* say he liked me. I think that a tanned me might just push him into snogging territory and thus get me the Ruaraidh Championship of the World, yay!

I didn't know what to say to make Holly feel better that wouldn't be giving up Ruaraidh, so I just said, "I'm sure you'll look much better tanned than I will. Dark-haired girls always do. I'm too fair for that."

She didn't look like she believed me an awful lot, but didn't say anything else. We found where the tanning sauces were kept (there were only three kinds), and looked them over.

"This one says it gives you a light, natural golden tan, "she said, holding up a bottle named Golden Sun Ease. "It lasts for three days and fades just like a real tan does."

I looked at it. "Eh. Looks wimpy. What we need is something that packs a bit of a wallop."

"Wallop? Will we look better walloped, or naturally golden?"

"Oh, you want to go with wallop whenever you can," I told her as I read another bottle. "I mean, you can't have too much of a tan, can you?"

"Well, I don't know. . . ."

"Sarah is *really* tanned. *Über*-tanned, I would say."

She sighed and put the Golden Sun Ease back on the shelf. "That's true. What do you have?"

I put it back. "Tropical Mist. Mists are good for perfume, but never for tans. You'd get all spotty with a tan mist and look like you had that horrible disease Brother is always going on about that medieval people had. You know, the one where parts of them like ears and fingers and nipples and stuff dropped off."

"Leprosy?"

"Yeah, that's it."

"I don't think people's nipples dropped off when they had leprosy."

I shrugged. "Doesn't matter, Brother said that it was really gruesome when someone got it. You don't want to look like a leper, do you? Spotty can't be an attractive look. What's that one called?"

She showed me the last tanning-sauce bottle. "Riviera Ultra Bronze."

"Oooh!" I picked up a bottle of it and read the back. " 'Tan at home without damaging your skin' . . . yadda yadda yadda . . . Hey, this sounds good! Listen: 'Ever wish you could look like you just returned from a week at Saint-Tropez? Now you can attain a gorgeous, deep, rich, dark Riviera tan in just a few seconds in the privacy of your own home. You can work out and swim without losing your tan—Riviera Ultra Bronze won't run, wash off, or fade for weeks.' Now that's what I'm talking about!"

Holly looked at the lady on the front of the bottle. "She's awfully dark, don't you think? She's kind of cocoa-colored."

"Naw, that's just because she's a blonde. Blondes tan darker. I'm getting some of this; it ought to work wonders. Ha! I'll show Ruaraidh who looks healthy!"

Holly looked back at the wimpy golden tan sauce. "Do you really think I would look OK with a Riviera tan rather than a light golden tan?"

"Sure, you would!"

She gnawed her lip a little. "Well . . ."

"OK, hands up, everyone here who's been to California."

She looked at me. I raised my hand. "California is the capital of the tanning world; everyone knows that. And I've been there, so I know what's what with tanning. Riviera Ultra Bronze is going to look much better on you than a blechy pale golden."

It took another ten minutes, but finally she saw reason and we both bought Riviera Ultra Bronze.

"I think I'm going to buy a couple of extra bottles," I told her as we went off to check out the nail polish selection (I wanted to find something that would go well with ultra-bronze).

"Extra? Why do we need extra?"

"It says you get a deeper tan by applying more, so we wouldn't want to run out. My mom tried some of this stuff once, and it was really weak and she had to use a lot before she got any color at all. And you've got dark hair and skin that looks like it'll take a lot of tanning sauce to make you Riviera Bronze. Don't worry; it'll be my treat. Mom called this morning and said she put some more money in my account."

She still looked a bit worried about the tanning sauce when we got home (and speaking of that, I had a little problem with the gate to the farm, but I'm going to ask Ruaraidh if he can find me some nails and white paint and wood, so I bet Alec won't even notice it).

"I'm just going to try a small area on the underside of my arm first, like the instructions recommend," Holly said when we were gathering up stuff for our tanning session.

"Fine, if you don't mind me looking gloriously Riviera Ultra Bronzed while you look all pasty and white and untanned. I'm going for maximum coverage."

She chewed her lip. "Well . . . maybe I should go for maximum, too."

"Sure, you should. Would I steer you wrong? It's just tanning cream; what can it hurt?"

She still looked worried when we marched downstairs to claim the bathroom as our tanning base camp. Alec watched us take in a couple of Aunt Tim's scented candles (aromatherapy), our skimpiest undies (I kind of wish I'd brought a swimsuit, but it's too cold here for that), my CD player and music (of course), a bunch of magazines, the brownies that Holly made earlier, the tanning lotions, nail polish so we could paint our toenails while we tanned, hair scrunchies (to keep our hair out of the sauce), five towels, and a couple of floor pillows.

As I was heading back to the bathroom with diet Coke, vanilla ice cream, and two glasses (you can't tan if you don't have floats!), I ran into Alec.

"Are you goin' to be in there for many weeks?" he asked,

looking into the bathroom, where Holly was arranging everything.

He was trying to be funny. I cut him a break because his accent is so hot and he's nummy and all. "No, but if you could move the phone and computer to the bathroom, I'd be really grateful."

He just looked at me.

"Joking!" I said, trying really hard not to roll my eyes, because even if he is ancient, he's still kind of cute.

"Do I want to know what it is they're doin' in there?" Alec asked Aunt Tim as I closed the bathroom door.

"No, you don't," she said, patting him on the arm. "It's girl stuff. It would just frighten you."

I would make fun of Aunt Tim saying that, but . . . well, what happened *was* kind of frightening. In a creepy sort of way. OK, in an awful, terrible, life-is-going-to-end sort of way.

Holly and I got all slathered up with tanning juice (she chickened out after all, putting on just a little bit, while I went for the deep Riviera look and used a whole bottle), and had floats and danced and stuff while we waited for our skin to go Riviera Ultra Bronze.

Only my skin didn't go bronze, ultra or otherwise. It went . . . orange.

Are you screaming yet?

"OHMICROD!" I yelled, spewing float out all over the bathroom mirror when Holly pointed out what was happening. "My skin matches the Copper Sunset Splendor part of my hair!"

"Here, wash it off," she said, handing me a washcloth, then grabbing a second one and soaping it up. "I'll help. It

123

hasn't been on too long, maybe it hasn't set yet. You don't think it's going to do that to me, do you?"

"*Wah!*" I yelled, and soaped up my arm while Holly scrubbed my leg, but the Riviera people weren't kidding when they said it wouldn't wash off. We used bar soap, antiseptic soap, shampoo, and finally the stuff with pumice in it that Aunt Tim leaves in the mudroom so people can wash up after being in the barn—all it did was make my orange tan redder.

"What am I going to do?" I said looking at myself in the mirror. I wanted to cry, I looked so terrible. Holly looked fine—she looked barely tanned—but I looked like a cross between an orange and a grapefruit. Even my *face* was orange! "I can't let anyone see me like this! OHMICROD! Ruaraidh! I'll die if he sees me like this!"

"Maybe there's something else we can try," Holly said, twisting a washcloth. "Maybe . . . I don't know, what about paint thinner?"

"Aaaaaaaaaaaack!" I yelled.

"Maybe we should ask your aunt—"

"Girls?" Aunt Tim knocked at the bathroom door. I looked at myself in the mirror, or what I could see of me in between the blobs of spit-out float and ice cream and streaks of diet Coke. I couldn't help it; tears started filling my eyes. "Are you all right? Alec said he heard screaming. I told him it was probably just you singing along to your music, but I thought I'd better—"

I swallowed hard and decided that nothing—other than Ruaraidh seeing me looking like Queen of the Orange People—could be as bad as what had happened, so I waved at Holly to unlock the door.

"—check and make sure . . . oh, my God, Emily . . . what

. . . what . . . dear heaven, you look like you have a pro-nounced case of jaundice. What happened?"

"It's the tanning stuff," I said, grabbing the box of tissues and mopping up my nose. "I think maybe I might have put . . . on . . . tooooooooo . . . mu-mu-much."

"Oh, Em." Aunt Tim hugged me, even the orange parts of me, then pushed back enough so she could look at my skin. "What did you use, furniture stain?"

Holly held out the bottle of the (stupid!) Riviera Ultra Bronze.

Aunt Tim looked at the orangey washcloths piled up in the sink. "It's not coming off?"

"Just a little did at first, but now all that happens when I try to scrub it off is that my skin hurts and turns red. This is it; I'm going to die. I know I said that before, but this time I really am. Can I borrow Alec's vet kit, please?"

Aunt Tim looked startled. "Why would you want that?"

I looked at myself in the mirror. I looked like a human-shaped orange Popsicle. "I'm going to put myself down."

She did a kinda sort of little laugh as she hugged me again, saying that it wasn't that bad; she was sure we'd be able to do something.

Because you're my BFF and I don't want to bore you to death, I won't tell you what she tried over the next half hour. Nothing worked. In the end she called the phone number listed on the bottle of tanning goober, but it was out of order, and when she called the chemist's to find out about them, they told her that the Rivera Ultra Bronze company had gone out of business due to consumer complaints!

Wah!

"I just talked to your mom," Aunt Tim said a while later. Holly and I were still in the bathroom—Holly was dressed now, and looking just fine with her pale golden tan, while I looked like Orangeina the circus freak. "She says you can go home if you'd like, although she's sure that the tan will fade pretty quickly if you scrub yourself a couple of times every day."

"Oh, Em," Holly said in a small little voice. "You don't want to go home, do you?"

"You wouldn't have to come with me," I answered, feeling awful. I did want to go home, which is stupid, isn't it? I mean, I'd still be orange when I got there! Only if I were home, Ruaraidh wouldn't see me.

She didn't say anything, just stood there squeezing her fingers and looking hopefully at me. Aunt Tim stood in the doorway. "It's your choice, kiddo. If you want to go home, we'll get you there."

I looked down at my orange legs. "Yeah, but what would I do about the work experience?"

I was kind of hoping she'd say that Alec would write me up the weekly reports even if I weren't here, but she didn't.

"You'll have to tell the school what happened."

"They won't give me credit if I do," I said, only a little bit pouty.

"No, I can't imagine they will."

"Great, so either I have to be the Amazing Orange Emily and get credit for WE, or I go home and they write on my transcript that I quit halfway through. Lovely. Wonderful."

"Emily, I don't mean to be unsympathetic, but this situation is of your own doing. You're almost an adult, honey. That means you have to take responsibility for your actions."

I glared at her. "I hate it when you do that!"

"Do what? Point out the obvious?"

I threw an orange-streaked towel at the bathtub. "No, make me feel like a little kid for wanting to hide." I looked over at Holly, still watching me with big, dark eyes. "OK, I'll stay. But this adult business isn't all it's cracked up to be."

Aunt Tim smiled, then leaned forward and kissed me on my forehead, which really *did* make me feel like a little kid. "Makeup?"

I looked in the mirror (Holly had cleaned it up while I was busy crying my eyes out). I nodded. "All of it. It's going to take every ounce of my skills to cover this up."

You're probably wondering how it turned out. Well, I'm still a bit on the orange side of the rainbow, but by putting a lot of foundation, powder, zit zapper, and concealer on my face, neck, and arms, at least I don't look like Orange Girl. Even though I made Aunt Tim promise she wouldn't say anything, I think she told Alec and Ruaraidh not to say anything about how I look, because when I finally left the bathroom—three hours after Holly and I went in—they just smiled and looked away really quickly without laughing or snorting or anything like that.

I caught Alec looking at me with squinty eyes this morning, but he didn't say anything, so maybe it doesn't show that much with all the makeup on.

So now I'm doomed to wearing long-sleeved shirts and pants. Aunt Tim is taking me to town this afternoon to see the local doctor just in case they have some sort of Riviera Ultra Bronze remover, and to buy a whole lot more concealer and powder.

When I get home, I'm going to have Brother sue the Riviera people. Aunt Tim says there's something you can get called punitive damages. Boy, have I been punitive! They're going to owe me *millions!*

Hugs and slightly orangeish kisses,
~Em

Subject: Crappidy crap crap crap!
From: Mrs.Legolas@kiltnet.com
To: Dru@seattlegrrl.com
Date: 16 January 2004 4:35pm

Alec noticed the gate. He says I'm grounded.
He can't do that, can he?

~Em the Orange

Subject: re: OHMICROD! ORANGE???
From: Mrs.Legolas@kiltnet.com
To: Dru@seattlegrrl.com
Date: 17 January 2004 8:51am

Dru wrote:
> Ohmicrod, I can't believe you did that! Don't you remem-
> ber me telling you about my cousin Donna, and how she
> did the same thing, and she got, like, blood poisoning or
> something from all the tanning stuff her skin soaked in?
> Not only did it dye her face, but her palms turned bright
> orange and all her eyelashes fell out. I went to see her a
> week afterward, and she looked *awful* with bare naked
> eyes and orange hands and yellowy skin. Geesh, Emily, I
> thought you would have remembered that!

Crap. Now I remember. I hate it when my brain forgets important stuff like that. Hang on; gotta go check something.

Back. I wanted to make sure my eyelashes weren't falling out, but they're OK, thank Crod. Can't write much 'cause as soon as Holly is out of the bathroom, it's my turn. We're going to Aberdeen today to see some sort of a dance-and-bagpipe show. Yeah, it sounds kinda lame-o, except Aunt Tim says there're always a bunch of cute guys there who hang around because of the girls, so I figured I'd go. I wasn't going to because of the Great Orange Incident, but Holly and Aunt Tim both swear that with my jacket and sweater and black jeans covering everything below my neck, and a lot of makeup above, no one will notice that I had a run-in with the Riviera people.

Oops, Holly's out. Later, chickadee!

Hugs and kissies,
~Em

Subject: re: Week Two Evaluation
From: Mrs.Legolas@kiltnet.com
To: Akrigon@gobottle.co.uk
Date: 17 January 2004 9:03pm

Akrigon wrote:
> was very pleased with the overall tone of the evaluation.
> Good job, Emily! One question— why did Mr. McGregor
> reference your artistic ability? I'm a little confused what
> you could find to be artistic about on a sheep farm. Signs,
> perhaps? Painting the barn?

> Best regards,
> Alan Krignon
> Headmaster, Gobottle School

I don't have to answer that, do I? I mean, if I do, it's not going on my official record or anything? Because not only do I want to get into a good university back home, but I want to be in one of the cool sororities, and my father says that the time he accidentally shaved his high school principal's dog's butt was somehow put on his school record, and kept him from getting into the cool frat house. You've met my father, so you can see what can happen if you have to go to a geeky frat because of some stupid little incident in your past.

Ciao,
Emily

Subject: re: Tomorrow is picture day!!!
From: Mrs.Legolas@kiltnet.com
To: Dru@seattlegrrl.com
Date: 17 January 2004 10:10pm

Dru wrote:
> I was going to get a perm, but you know how iffy they
> can be, and besides, they're always so permy the first few
> days. I don't want to look like I got a perm; I just want
> naturally curly hair.

You'll look gorgeous; will you stop fussing? If you just do the hot rollers, you'll knock his socks off; I guarantee it. And no, I don't think you should go with the Pink look. I mean, if you absolutely insist that the standard Dru look of coolio-ness is not going to cut it, go with the Christina Aguilera look. That's sexy without being slutty.

> Is your orange fading yet? Can you go out in public with-
> out making people stare?

You know what? I think it *is* starting to fade, although Aunt Tim said the woman at the chemist's says it's not supposed to, but I think Mom was right—I scrub my skin with a loofah every morning and night, and I think I'm a little less orangey.

But I'm still going to get Brother to sue the Riviera people. If I didn't have that coolio thing down pat, this could have *ruined* my life!

So, as you've probably guessed, we're back from Aberdeen. Alec refused to let us go to the big mall in the center of town, which I thought was awfully stinky of him until Aunt Tim said that if Devon and Fang come up early next weekend, we can all go to the big mall in Inverness. She said there's a big one with all sorts of really hip shops, as well as a smaller Victorian shopping center. Must remember to write to Fang and Dev next and tell them to leave really early, because I'm abso-positively *starved* for a good mall!

The Scottish dancing thing was OK, lots of girls dancing around with swords and frilly shirts and stuff. There weren't as many guys there as Aunt Tim said there would be, but it was still OK. Holly and I were doing guys-in-kilts checks for the ones that were there, but when one of them slipped on a bit of ice outside . . . OHMICROD! Do you *know* what guys wear under their kilts? I'll give you a hint—it starts with N and ends with G and has OTHIN in the middle! Holly almost fainted when she saw the kilt guy slip. I felt bad for him for slipping and probably getting a pretty bodacious booty burn on the ice, but just think about it—wool itches! Can you imagine wearing it on your bare butt? Itch city!

Anyhoo, back to our day. Ruaraidh . . . sigh. I really think that my experience with Aidan has damaged me. Picture the scene: we're walking through this hall place where the dancing is going on (that's Aunt Tim and Alec, Ruaraidh, and Holly and me), and Ruaraidh is looking *über-*snogalicious in his black leather jacket and black jeans. Since I'm still a bit on the O side, I wore my chinos and black silk shirt, with a really subtle makeup since I read in *Vogue* that subtle was v. in for days, while dramatic should be kept for night only. Anyway, as we were walking through the big hall place, Ruaraidh's hand brushed against mine.

You know, of course, what that means. He wanted to hold my hand! OK, I know, one hand brush is not absolute evidence, but two hand brushes is, and that's what he did! As we were walking his hand brushed against mine *again!*

This is why I think the thing with Aidan has damaged me. Instead of doing a little hand brush to him, indicating that I was willing to hold hands with him if he took my hand first, I pretended I had to stop and tie my shoelace, and when I was done, I went over onto the other side of Holly rather than next to Ruaraidh!

What do you think that means? I tried to figure it all out, but all I can think of is that it has to be that:

- I just think I like him because he's all nummy and stuff, but I really don't, only I don't know that I don't like him.
- I *do* like him, but I didn't want to hold his hand because it has six fingers, which would mean that I really don't like

him, because if you like someone, you like them despite weirdo things like their having six fingers.
- I like him OK, but not enough to be holding his hand in front of everyone.
- I like him a lot and want to snog his lips right off his head, but don't want to hurt Holly by having her see him holding my hand when he doesn't want to hold hers.
- I don't like him and know it, and don't want him holding my hand (this doesn't seem right because I feel like I like him, but you know, after that whole Aidan thing, I'm not quite sure if *thinking* you like someone is the same as *really* liking them. Oh, never mind; it's too confusing).

So what do you think? I need to know what it means, because Ruaraidh smiled a lot at me while we were in Aberdeen, and sat next to me in a booth when Alec and Aunt Tim took us to dinner (pizza! Yay!). His leg touched mine a couple of times, and leg touches are *much* more meaningful than hand brushes, don't you think?

Meh. Going to bed. I'm too tired to figure it all out. Tell me everything about Brent and the pictures! And don't do Pink! That look is all wrong for you!

Hugsies and kissies,
~Em

Subject: Um.
From: Mrs.Legolas@kiltnet.com
To: BessWill@btinternet.co.uk
Date: 19 January 2004 9:43am

Hey, Bess, I have one of those, whaddya call 'em, rhetorical questions for you. What do you think it means when a guy does two hand brushes and three thigh touches, but the touchee doesn't really want to hold his hand or play thighsies? Does it mean the touchee doesn't really like him because she knows that despite being a megahottie who seems nice, he's really no different from, say, another megahottie who turned out to be a major poophead?

Or does it mean that the touchee is just a bit weirded out after her last experience with the poophead, and really there's nothing wrong with the megahottie at all?

Emily

Subject: re: Dev says yes
From: Mrs.Legolas@kiltnet.com
To: Fbaxter@oxfordshire.agricoll.co.uk
Date: 19 January 2004 9:59am

Fbaxter wrote:
> so we'll be up late Saturday afternoon, probably around
> tea. You're sure your aunt won't mind us staying two
> days? I don't mind going to the mall with you, so long as
> you don't make me look at shoes. I'll never understand
> the fascination girls have with shoes.

Yay! I'm so glad you guys are coming up early so we can go malling in Inverness on Sunday. Aunt Tim says the two malls there are really fabu, and I swear I won't take you into any shoe stores, although you have to promise to wait outside when Holly and Devon and I go into them, because shoes are just, like, *so* important! They can make a whole outfit! Guys have feet, too, and I just don't understand why you don't recognize the importance of fabulous footwear.

Anyway, I'll see you on Saturday! It'll be just like a slumber party, except we won't paint each other's toenails.

I will braid your hair for you, if you want me to. Hahahahahahah!

Big smoochy kissies,
Emily

Subject: re: My life is over. *Completely over!*
From: Mrs.Legolas@kiltnet.com
To: Dru@seattlegrrl.com
Date: 19 January 2004 4:13pm

Dru wrote:
> waited for *a whole hour* but he never showed up! I could
> just die of the embarrassment! There were other people
> wandering around the park, and I was sure they thought
> I was some loser girl whose date stood her up, because
> they started to give me *pity looks!* Oh, Crod!

OK, let's examine this terrible situation and see what you can salvage out of it. First of all, you shouldn't be embarrassed at all; you didn't do anything wrong. *You* didn't make a date with a girl to take her picture and then not show up. You're innocent in all this, and I say you play up the victim angle instead of feeling bad because you temporarily got sucked in by a total and complete poop. Think drama queen here. It's better than hiding in your bedroom and refusing to come out! Besides, I don't think your coach is going to be happy if you miss many more days at school. You don't want to get kicked off the swim team just because of Brent the Poop, now, do you? I didn't think so.

> I want to die; I just want to die. I'm never going to be
> able to face anyone again. I told everyone, *everyone!*
> Heather and Pam and Lissa and Sukie, and they'll all
> laugh at me because that stupid, stupid, *stupid* Brent
> dumped me!

Well, Heather will probably be kind of snotty to you about it; you know what a witch she can be about guys. But Pam and Lissa and Sukie will all stand behind you, and no, I don't think they'll be secretly laughing behind your back. They're your friends, stupid! Friends don't do that. Friends side with you every time, even if you're wrong. That's what friendship is all about!

Oh, geez, that made me think of Holly. Gotta go; Alec wants to see the database again tonight, and I'm behind on entering the dull, dull, dull sheep data.

This should cheer you up!

Emily's Hottie of the Week

Hottie #2—Devon Eliott

[If you go to the Web site, you'll see a picture of Devon in his knight's outfit.]

- Name: Devon Alexander Eliott
- Birthdate: February 6, 1985
- Height: 6'0"
- Famous for: flirty way with girls, and scrumdillyicious knight costume
- Skateboarding skill: doesn't skateboard, prefers surfing Aruba instead
- Can he shoot a bow and arrow: hasn't tried it, but I'm sure he could if he wanted to
- Does he look good in tights: drool city!
- Does he look good in a blond wig: has blond tips on hair and it looks fabu
- Coolness rating: eight out of ten pointy ears (minus two ears for dating more than one girl at the same time)
- Surf or motorcycle: both!
- Chest test: $19
- Dream date: concert, then clubbing, then romantic dinner where he stares into my eyes and tells me that he can't think of anyone else and swears his love for me forever
- Boxers or briefs: the little teeny, tiny briefs that come in hot colors and are scrunched up really small into cute boxes
- Orli rating: 92

Big squeezy hugs,
~Em

Subject: re: You don't care what happens to me
From: Mrs.Legolas@kiltnet.com
To: Dru@seattlegrrl.com
Date: 19 January 2004 4:19pm

Dru wrote:
> Oh, fine, you just go do your hottie stuff and your sheep
> database and just forget about the fact that I'm sitting in
> my bedroom dying of mortification!

You're not dying, Dru. And I do too care what happens to you—you're my BFF—but I've got to stop doing e-mail and do the sheep stuff or else Alec won't write me a good evaluation. So go get some ice cream and watch old *Buffy* shows and I'll be back as soon as I can,'kay?

Hugs and kisses,
~Em

Subject: re: Life sucks!
From: Mrs.Legolas@kiltnet.com
To: Dru@seattlegrrl.com
Date: 19 January 2004 4:23pm

Dru wrote:
> I'm never coming out of my room again, and then I'll get
> kicked off the swim team and I won't get that scholarship,
> which means I won't be able to go to UCLA, and I'll end
> up working at Dairy Queen and get pimples from working
> the fryer and no guy will *ever* want to date me *ever* be-
> cause I'll be such a loser, and it'll all be *your fault* because
> you couldn't be bothered to help me, your BFF, when I

> needed your help! I hope you're happy; I just hope you're
> happy!

Boy, you're really taking that drama-queen stuff to
heart, aren't you?
I'll be back later. Promise.

Hugs and kisses,
~Em

Subject: re: Well . . .
From: Mrs.Legolas@kiltnet.com
To: Dru@seattlegrrl.com
Date: 19 January 2004 4:24pm

Dru wrote:
> You promise you'll e-mail me later?

I promise! Now go take a shower. I bet you haven't taken
one yet, and you probably stink and stuff. You know how
sweaty you get when you cry.

Hs and Ks,
~Em

Subject: re: OK.
From: Mrs.Legolas@kiltnet.com
To: Dru@seattlegrrl.com
Date: 19 January 2004 4:25pm

Dru wrote:
> I do not stink! I'm just a bit . . . um . . . sticky. That's not
> the same as stinking! I'm going to take a shower now,
> but remember what you promised. I can't get through
> this awful day if you don't make me laugh and tell me
> how evil Brent is, and make me feel better about calling
> Heather and telling her what happened.

Just remember, the only difference between stinky and
sticky is one letter.
No, I don't know what that means. Meh.

~Em who is really, really, really going to stop reading e-
mail now

Subject: You are not going to *believe* what happened!
From: Mrs.Legolas@kiltnet.com
To: Dru@seattlegrrl.com
Date: 22 January 2004 8:03am

We are talking major OMICROD here, grrl! I'm still all
weirded out and stuff, but I feel a bit . . . well, freaked! Kind
of. And kind of happy. In a freaked sort of way.
Here's what happened—last night we were all sitting
around watching TV. Well, Holly and I were, and Alec and
Aunt Tim were in the sitting room reading and listening to

the radio, and Ruaraidh was on the phone talking to his mom. Holly was finishing up her sweater. She's almost done with it! Can you believe that? She's almost done even though she's been sick for the last two days with a bad cold. I have to admit, her sweater looks pretty good. It has different colors and stripes and stuff. I'd be jealous except for what happened.

So anyway, there Holly and I were, watching *Pop Idol* (it's an English version of *American Idol*) and making fun of the singers.

"You know, you have a really good voice; you could go on there," I told Holly. "You'd make lots of money and have tons of guys drooling over you."

She stopped blowing her nose and looked horrified, really scared. "I couldn't! I couldn't ever do that!"

"Sure, you could. I bet it's easy. I'll look at their Web site later and see what you have to do to get on there."

"No, Emily, please don't," she said, and tugged on my sleeve, which was really kind of pathetic, but I didn't want to tell her so because she was still sick and everything. "I don't want to sing."

"OK, but it's a shame, because you have a v. good voice. Hey, how does this look?" I held up the sweater I was knitting for Ruaraidh (no stripes and only one color).

Holly's eyes watered and she started coughing when she looked at it, but I'm sure that was her cold. I mean, there really wasn't anything wrong with my sweater. Other than the fact that one arm was about four inches shorter than the other. And there were a couple of holey spots where something weird had happened. And the edges curled up and I couldn't get them to uncurl. But other than that it was fine.

"So what do you think, will Ruaraidh like it?"

I had to wait a few minutes for her to stop coughing, but once she swigged down some hot tea and honey, she could speak. "I'm sure he'll love it. It's so very . . . unique."

I stroked my hand down the front. I knew it wasn't perfect, but it was still v. cool that I could knit at all, considering I'd never done it before. "Yeah, well, it doesn't have to be as good as yours, I just want to make something that Ruaraidh will like, and this . . . What are they *doing*?"

Aunt Tim and Alec had been listening to music, old-people stuff like the Eagles and Linda Ronstadt, but all of a sudden the music changed over to Latin music, and got a whole lot louder. I put down my sweater and trotted out to see what happened, Holly following behind me.

Ruaraidh was just coming out of the kitchen when the door to the sitting room was thrown open, and Alec and Aunt Tim danced out of the room and down the hallway toward the kitchen.

Danced! Right there in front of us! And Aunt Tim was giggling!

"Um. What are you doing?" I asked as Holly and I followed them into the kitchen.

"The tango!" Aunt Tim said.

Oh, right. I guess old people are sometimes overcome with the desire to tango.

"It's fun," she said as Alec twirled her around the kitchen table. "Try it!"

I looked at Holly. She looked at me. We both turned back to look at Aunt Tim and Alec. "We don't know how, and isn't it, like, an old people's dance?"

"No, it's very hot and steamy. Only very sexy people dance it. Maybe it's a bit too old for you," she said, and tangoed past us back toward the sitting room where tango music was blaring out the door.

Too old for us? Ha!

"OK, so how do you do this tango thing?" I asked as they came tangoing back into the kitchen. It didn't look hard, and I had to admit, Aunt Tim was plastered up pretty close to Alec. I could see where it might be a v. sexy dance to do. I eyed Ruaraidh. "I want to try."

"It's very easy," Aunt Tim said. "Just step, step, step, twirl. Ruaraidh, do you know how to tango?"

Ruaraidh had been leaning against the kitchen sink watching Alec and Aunt Tim. "No, but it looks fun." He stood up and held his hands out to me. "Come on, Emily; let's give it a try."

I looked at Holly, but she had a blanket draped around her and was obviously too sick to dance. She sat down on a stool and gave me a weak smile.

"Step, step, step, twirl," I said as I took Ruaraidh's hands. He pulled me up close, and after watching AT and Alec for a minute, started step, step, step, twirling. The only problem is that while he twirled, I was stepping, and we both ended up on the floor.

"You all right?" Ruaraidh asked as he helped me to my feet. Aunt Tim and Alec stopped dancing and came over to us.

"Yeah, but I don't think we were doing something right."

"You're not putting the action into your hips," Aunt Tim said, then put her hands on Ruaraidh's hips to make him swivel (it sounds pervy, but it wasn't). "Your hips, Ruaraidh, hips! You're too stiff. You have to have loose hips to tango correctly. Here, watch Alec; he has wonderfully loose hips."

Alec and Aunt Tim tangoed around Ruaraidh and me.

"You see? The tango is the dance of hot, sultry love. You have to ooze sexuality when you dance it. Just remember to keep your hips loose, both of you."

"You game for another try?" Ruaraidh asked with a grin that used to make my stomach go all fluttery but now it didn't. "Your hips nice and loose?"

"Sure," I said, "but I don't want to loosen them too much, or a leg will drop off."

He laughed and I waited for the happy "Ruaraidh is laughing at something I said, go me!" feeling to start, but it didn't. So we step, step, step, twirled a couple of times until we were pretty much tangoing, although we weren't as good as Alec and Aunt Tim.

It was fun, Dru! I know it sounds totally grotty and all, but it really was fun. I got to squish up next to Ruaraidh while we were hot and sultry and oozed sexuality (even if he didn't make me go fluttery any more, the squishing was fun), and even Holly smiled as we danced around her. Alec offered to show her how to tango, but she started coughing after only step, step, with no twirl, so she ended up just watching us. Ruaraidh really got into it and was very loose-hipped, and I have to say it was abso-fabulously coolio when he wrapped his arms around my waist and really let his hips go to town. He was rubbing all over me, but it was part of the dance, so evidently it was OK. I did glance at Aunt Tim a couple of times when Ruaraidh did a couple of bendy-over backward moves, but she didn't seem to think anything about it. Of course, she and Alec were sneaking kisses when they thought we weren't looking, so they were obviously flirting with each other big-time.

We tangoed around the kitchen, down the hall, and through the sitting room and dining room, then back to the kitchen until we couldn't catch our breaths. Just as we stopped, Ruaraidh's hands slid down onto my butt, and he touched cheek! While I was smooshed up against him! He smiled at me while he was doing it, too, which pretty much made it official—he was obviously hot for me. Don't you think? Or do you think it was just an accidental touch? He didn't squeeze or anything. No, I think he did it on purpose.

Holly didn't see the butt touch, and since she was sick and all, I didn't think it was right to flirt with Ruaraidh right there in front of her, so I just backed away from him without saying anything. A couple of minutes later Alec turned off the tango music, and he and Ruaraidh went out do whatever they do out in the barn to put the animals to bed. Holly went up to bed, and I took a shower so I could do my nightly scrub-off-the-orange-and-return-Emily's-skin-to-normal ritual.

"It looked like you were having a lot of fun dancing," Holly said later, after I'd gotten into my baby-doll and was sitting on the edge of my bed trying to decide if I wanted my toenails Ravening Red or Beach Bum Pink.

I waved a bottle of nail polish at her. "Well, you know that I have v. high standards when it comes to dancing—I mean, if you aren't cool while you're doing it, you look like you're having a spazz attack—but I have to admit that the tango can be mondo tight. If you've got a good partner, of course. It's too bad you didn't get to dance, too. You OK?"

She'd started to cough while I was speaking. I waited until she was done and then asked her if she wanted more cough syrup.

"No, but . . ." She shivered under the bedspread. "Do you think you could get me another cup of tea? With honey and lemon?"

"Sure, NP. You want me to ask Aunt Tim to look at you? I heard her and Alec come upstairs; she's probably not in bed yet."

Holly shivered and burrowed deeper beneath the blankets until just her bangs, eyes, and nose peeked out. "No, just the tea. My throat is kind of hurty and the tea makes it feel better."

" 'Kay I'll be right back."

I got into my comfy moose slippers—did I tell you about them? My grandma sent them to me for Christmas. They're silly, I know, but v. fun. The front of the slipper is shaped like a moose head, and has big brown antlers that poke out. The slippers make this low *mmmmmoo* noise with every step. I think it's supposed to be what a moose says, although I doubt if they really say that. Anyway, I moosed up my feet and trotted off downstairs to heat up some water for Holly.

You know how it is when everyone in the house is asleep and you go downstairs and it's all dark and stuff? You know, that kind of scary darkness that makes you sure there's an ax murderer hiding in a corner? Well, it was like that. I ran down the hallway to the kitchen, my slippers *mmmmmoo*-ing wildly, and threw myself through the kitchen door before any of the axmurderers could get me, but it turns out everyone wasn't in bed like I thought.

"Aaaaaaaaaack!" I screamed when Ruaraidh loomed up out of the dark dining room. He jumped and clutched his chest for a minute before coming forward.

"Fekkin' A, you gave me a fright. I thought everyone was upstairs. . . ." His voice trailed off as he eyed me up and down. I suddenly realized that since I was in my baby-doll, my arms and legs were bare, which meant he could see the

Riviera Ultra Orange. Eek! "Erm. Those are . . . uh . . . very interesting slippers."

I thought about turning around and running back upstairs, but it was too late. He'd seen my orange skin. I just hoped that because I'd been scrubbing faithfully with the loofah twice a day, and because the dim light over the stove was the only thing on in the kitchen, maybe he wouldn't notice and would think I was just really tanned.

"Oh, yeah, they are. They talk."

"Ah." He set his boots down and peeled off his jacket. "I've been meaning to ask you, who's winning the contest?"

"The contest?" I asked, my blood freezing solid in horror. OHMICROD, he knew about the contest!

"Yes, the contest. Who's ahead?"

"How do you know about the contest?" For one teensy minute I thought maybe Holly had ratted on me in order to gain an advantage, but immediately I felt bad about thinking that because Holly wouldn't cheat.

"Maybe it was the way you've been trying to get my attention," he said with a grin that would have made me go all girly if I wasn't frozen into a horrified block of embarrassment. "Or maybe it was the fact that you and Holly both try to do things to please me."

That's it. My life is over.

"Or the fact that you're knitting me a sweater."

Really over. No life. None. Whatsoever.

"Or maybe it was the big wall chart labeled *2004 Who Snogs Ruaraidh First Challenge* that shows the points for both you and Holly."

In fact, I'm now officially dead. I've died and am now in hell.

Ruaraidh just stood there halfway in the shadows, wearing a black shirt and pants, looking all droolworthy and mysterious, and all of a sudden I knew—I positively knew—he was going to kiss me. It was in his eyes. It was in the way he glided toward me. It was in the air, it was everywhere! HE WAS GOING TO KISS ME!

He leaned forward (it was coming!), put his hands on my arms (he was going to kiss me!), squeezed lightly (I would win the snogging contest!), then his lips parted (THIS WAS IT!). "Don't you think the whole contest thing is a bit silly? It's flattering and all, but you're both a bit too young for me."

I blinked a couple of times. OK, I blinked a gazillion times, and do you know what? Blinking doesn't really help your mind work any better. I thought it might like get more oxygen to it or something, but it didn't, because I just stood there staring at him, in the About To Be Kissed Pose #4, and all I could say was, "Too young? Holly and me? Are you *insane*?"

"Well, you might be old enough, but Holly's really still just a little girl," he said, squeezing my arms one more time before he let them go.

In that moment I saw that I had been right about him all along—he wasn't as nice as I first thought he was. Oh, he was nummy-looking, and fun and stuff, but in the end, he was just a guy who only thought about himself, just like Aidan. And you know what? That made me mad, mucho mega mondo mad! I could live with the fact that he was making fun of our contest, but how dare he pick on Holly when she's come so far in the last few months?

I straightened my shoulders and gave him my best squinty eyes. "Holly is the most mature person I know. She's smart, and she loves animals, and she's funny, and everyone loves her."

Ruaraidh gave me a lop-sided smile. "I know that, I like her, too, but I reckoned she was too young to date, otherwise I would have asked her out."

"Too young? Ha! She's got guys falling all over her back home," I told him, lying through my teeth, yes, but it was a good lie, a kind lie. I couldn't let him think Holly was a baby!

He looked surprised. "She does?"

"Tons of guys. She has to beat them off with her field hockey stick, there're so many. And they all like her because she's so much fun to be around. And she likes animals, and . . . and . . ." That's when it hit me. There I was, standing in the almost dark in my baby-doll, telling Ruaraidh just how wonderful Holly was, and he was really listening to me because HE LIKED HER MORE THAN HE LIKED ME!

"Do you think she'd fancy going to a club with me?"

I looked at him standing there all nummy and hottalicious and gorgeous and stuff, trying to remember just how much fun I had tangoing with him, and how much I liked him at first, and how badly I wanted to win the contest, but honestly, Dru, all I could think about was Holly. I took a deep breath and stepped back until I was near the kitchen door. "I think she'd love it."

"Hmm," he asked, standing there looking so good. He rubbed his chin. "Guess I'll ask her out, then."

"You do that," I said, and took another step toward the door.

He crossed his arms over his chest and tipped his head to the side. "She's only fifteen, though, isn't she?"

I nodded my head and felt for the door behind me.

"I've never had a girlfriend that young. But she *does* like animals." He raised his eyebrows at me like he was asking me something.

"Loves them," I answered, just wanting to get out of there so I could think about things. "And she's a very *old* fifteen. She'll be sixteen in less than half a year."

"Oh. Well then, I guess it's good we talked. Thanks, Emily."

"She really likes you, too," I said, because guys like to know you like them.

He grabbed his jacket from the chair and started toward me. I backed up until I hit the wall next to the door. "Yeah, I know. Thanks. Night, then."

He walked out of the kitchen. I waited until I heard him go up the stairs, then I slid down the wall and sat on the floor, half of me feeling weak, the other half wanting to laugh. He wanted Holly! Holly wanted him! Yeah, it stung a little that he liked her more than me, but I think that whole thing with Aidan has given me like a guy vaccination or something, because it really didn't hurt that much.

I just kept thinking how happy Holly was going to be, and that made me feel happy, too. Yeah, I still had orange-ish skin, and Alec wasn't thrilled with me because I hadn't finished the database when I said I would, and I'd just been turned down by a (new status: former) Scottish God of Love, but all in all, I felt pretty good.

After a few minutes I got Holly's tea and took it upstairs, and before you ask, no, I didn't say anything to her, I just gave her the tea and got into bed. I didn't want to hurt her feelings by telling her that Ruaraidh thought she was too young until I talked him into giving her a chance.

I feel *just* like one of those saints and martyrs and people who do good deeds.

Oops. Holly just got up. Her cold is better but Alec said she should stay inside for a few days. Let me know what you think when you get up.

Hugs and kisses,
Saint Emily

Subject: re: You're dating three boys?
From: Mrs.Legolas@kiltnet.com
To: Hwilliams@mediev-l.oxford.co.uk
Date: 23 January 2004 8:20pm

Hwilliams wrote:
> Timandra says you've rounded up a whole gang of boys
> to go with you to Inverness. I just want to remind you
> that despite your mother thinking you're old enough to
> make these sorts of decisions on your own, anything of
> an even remotely sexual nature is yet another nail in my
> coffin. Just think of my weak heart when you get those
> primal, consuming urges I know you teenage girls get.
> Oh, for a good chastity belt.

Excuse me, do I know you? I believe you e-mailed me by mistake, total and complete utter stranger. Please remove me from your address book. I think this qualifies as spam, and under the international spam laws, I'm not legally obligated to listen to sex advice via e-mail.
'Bye!

Sex Kitten Emily

Subject: Holly Update
From: Mrs.Legolas@kiltnet.com
To: Dru@seattlegrrl.com
Date: 23 January 2004 9:11pm

Just a quickie, because Holly wants me to go over her clothes and show her what to wear, and also to do a total makeover on her, and you know that can take hours. When she went upstairs after dinner, she was all glowy and smiley and stuff.

"You look like you're feeling a lot better," I said. You know how observant I am about things. "I take it you're not hacking up greeners anymore?"

"No, I'm much better. But you'll never guess what just happened," she said, smiling really big. She grabbed Julian and did a little dance around the room.

"OK, what happened?" I asked.

"Guess!"

I set down my apricot facial scrub (I really think it's work- ing on taking the orange out of my face) and gave her a Look. "I hate that game. I never guess right, so you just tell me."

"Ruaraidh asked me if I wanted to go to the circus with him. Like on a date. Me! I was sure he was going to ask you, but he didn't; he asked me."

It was on the tip of my tongue to tell her what happened, but as soon as I saw how sparkly her eyes were, I remem- bered that I was being Saint Emily and all, and that meant I couldn't tell her the truth because it would really hurt her feelings. So all I said was, "Oh, good."

She stopped dancing and looked over to me, her face all frowny. "You don't mind, do you? If you didn't want me to go with him, I wouldn't, Em. You're my best friend forever, and if you don't want me to go with Ruaraidh—"

"Me?" I gave a little laugh, which really proves I am one of those saints, because I was feeling just a teeny, tiny bit hurt even though I didn't want to date Ruaraidh. "No, I don't mind. After all, Devon and Fang will be here tomorrow, and you know I really like them both."

"Do you like one of them . . . that way?"

I took a deep breath and looked over to where I'd put Devon's knight picture next to my personally signed Orlando picture. "That's hard to say. I mean, it's not hard because . . . well, it's hard."

"Emily," she said, tossing Julian and coming over to sit on the bed next to me. "You don't . . . you're not . . . is one of them your crush?"

I gathered up the apricot scrub, cucumber toner, and moisturizer. "All I'll say is that I'm going to be very happy to see Devon . . . and Fang, of course."

"Ooooh." Her eyes went all wide for a second; then she did that big smile again. "I'm so glad you're not mad because Ruaraidh prefers me to you! I was worried that you would be, but then I knew that you're my true friend, and true friends are always happy for their BFFs. This is going to be such a wonderful weekend!"

She started dancing around the room again, and I got my towel and went off to do the nightly face stuff. And before you ask, no, Devon isn't my crush, although he is very hot and I really like him. I just said that so Holly wouldn't give up Ruaraidh because of me. I like Devon and all, but he's so flirty! It would be different if he could be with just one girl, but he always seems to have great big herds of girls around him.

Still, I'll have two guys when she's only got one. Although neither of mine are BFs, and hers will be. And hers is a Scottish god of love. Or, he used to be, now he's just . . . um . . . Scottish.

Sigh. This martyr stuff isn't all it's cracked up to be.

Hugs and kisses,
~Em

Subject: re: My heart is broken, but I'm not stupid!
From: Mrs.Legolas@kiltnet.com
To: Dru@seattlegrrl.com
Date: 24 January 2004 7:58am

Dru wrote:
> just because I was *cruelly* and *horribly* dumped by that
> evil Brent who tried to ruin my life doesn't mean that I
> can't ever again go out. And I know I said that Tim was
> a bit geeky, but I've decided that there's safety in geeki-
> ness, and it's better to have a geeky BF than no BF. So,
> I'm going to see *Return of the King* with Tim, even
> though he's, like, the biggest Tolkien dweeb in the whole
> wide world. I just hope he doesn't wear pointy ears this
> time.

I happen to think he's kind of cute, but in a non-BF sort of way. I also think you're making abso-tively the right decision. See? I told you drama queen would work for you. Now everyone feels sorry for you in a good way (as opposed to feeling superior to you, which is just too ghastly for words), and they're all trying to find BFs for you so your broken heart will be whole again. Have fun at *ROTK*. Holly and I saw it four days in a row right after it opened, and all I can say is it's slobbersville! Leggy rocks!

Today is Devon and Fang day! They're coming up this afternoon so we can go into Inverness early tomorrow and mall before we go over to the Circus of the Darned. Oh! Get this! Evidently this Burns-night thing here in Scotland is a majorly big deal, and you have to make this sheep dinner called *haggis* to celebrate it. Since we're all going to be in Inverness seeing the circus tomorrow night, Aunt Tim said we could do the dinner tonight, only she caught Holly's cold. Then Holly (she's much better, thanks for asking) said that we'd do it, so now she and I have to cook. Actual food! For people! I know; it scares me, too. I mean, I'm fine using the microwave, but you know what happened that time we tried to make tacos. I'm just glad your cat's hair grew back.

Gotta run. I have to go look up the recipe for haggis. Holly's going to do the dessert and the munchies, and I get the main part of dinner because Aunt Tim says it all cooks together.

Glad you are feeling happy again!

Hugs and kisses,
~Em

Subject: It's just *Too icky for words*!!!
From: Mrs.Legolas@kiltnet.com
To: Dru@seattlegrrl.com
Date: 24 January 2004 9:31am

I am so shocked, I almost can't speak! Well, OK, I guess technically I'm not talking, I'm typing, but you know what I mean. A little bit ago, after I was done e-mailing you, I went downstairs to breffie to see what I had to do to make this haggis stuff. Oh. My. Crod. You are *not* going to believe what it is! I would have thought everyone was pulling my leg, but they all looked serious, and when I cornered Holly after brekkers and asked her if it was a joke, she said no, and Holly never lies!

These people in Scotland are just plain weird!

"So," I said, sitting down with my scorched pancake (Alec was cooking because Aunt Tim was all coldish). "What's the deal on this Burns dinner thing?"

Aunt Tim sneezed. "It's a supper in honor of Robert Burns, the poet. The haggis is cooked with neeps and tatties—which is mashed turnips and potatoes—and then brought to the table while the Burns poem is recited."

"What poem?" I asked.

" 'Fair fa' your honest, sonsie face, Great chieftain o' the puddin'-race! Aboon them a' ye tak your place, Painch, tripe, or thairm: Weel are ye wordy of a grace, As lang's my arm.' " (I looked it up, in case you were wondering.)

I looked over at Alec. "Um. What language was that?"

He laughed.

"It's kind of a mixture of Scots and English," Aunt Tim said, blowing her noise. "It's part of the 'Address to a Haggis,' the poem Burns wrote about his love for haggis."

I rolled my eyes. I mean, I love pizza more than anything in this world, but I don't write poems to it. "OK, so I cook the sheep and mashed potatoes and turnips, which sounds gross, but whatever, and then you recite this poem. That's it?"

Aunt Tim looked at Alec. He grinned at her, then put a plate of pancakes on the table. "Haggis isn't mutton, Emily. It's . . . er . . . more than that."

"What do you mean, more than that? You mean the taps and neeties?"

"Neeps and tatties," Alec said. Aunt Tim choked on her coffee. "Would you be likin' to tell her, love?"

"No," Aunt Tim wheezed. "You're doing just fine. Go ahead. Get it over with. You know it's better that way."

I looked from Aunt Tim to Alec, then to Holly, who looked just as confused as I felt. "What? I told you I wasn't a very good cook, so if it's something fancy, I don't want to do it."

Alec took a deep breath, then said, really fast, "Haggis is made up of a sheep's heart, lungs, liver, suet, oatmeal, onions, and spices, all boiled in a sheep's stomach."

I stared at Alec in horror for a moment, then jumped back from the table. *"Ew! Ew ew ew ew ew!"*

Holly looked like she was going to ralph up her pancake. Aunt Tim sighed. "It's not really that bad—"

"Ew!" I said again, feeling all creepy. "A heart? Lungs? Liver? *In the stomach???"*

Alec shrugged, and shoveled a forkful of pancake into his mouth. " 'Tis a traditional meal."

"Traditional, schmaditional, this girl does not cook sheep guts! Ewie gross!"

"You don't have to cook it, Emily," Aunt Tim said tiredly.

"We can get one precooked at the grocery store. All you'll have to do is warm it up."

Ruaraidh walked in just then, and it just goes to show you how grossed out I was, because I stood there staring at Aunt Tim with my mouth hanging open right in front of him.

"You are, like, *so* completely insane if you think I'm going to even get near something so icky as that!"

"What's icky?" Ruaraidh asked, poking his fork into the pancake stack and taking a bunch of them.

"Haggis," Holly answered, because she was his almost-GF.

"Haggis? There's nothing icky about it."

You see what would have happened if I had wanted Ruaraidh as a BF? I'd have to dump him, because there is no way in the world I could ever kiss a guy who ate sheep's innards in a stomach. *Blech!*

"Well, I don't care what you guys eat," I said, sitting back down to my pancake, although I gave it a good hard look to make sure Alec didn't slip any sheep organs into it, "but I can tell you right here and now that I'm not eating it. I'll have pizza, thank you."

Alec frowned. "It's traditional to eat haggis on Burns Night—"

"Oh, Alec, don't bother. It's all right, girls. When you go to the store to pick up the haggis, you can get yourselves a pizza. Better make it two. Perhaps Fang and Devon won't be into traditional Scottish fare, either." Aunt Tim turned to me. "If Holly warms up the haggis and does the neeps and tatties, do you think you could do the soup? It's cock-a-leekie."

I jumped up from the table and threw—positively *threw*—

down my napkin. "I do *not* want to know what part of a sheep goes into *that*!"

Then I ran away, because you know, a girl can only take so much ick at breakfast.

BTW, Aunt Tim told me later that cock-a-leekie soup is made with chickens, not sheep's thingies, like I thought.

Off to the store to buy the sheep barf in a bag for the weirder members of the family, and pizza for those of us who are normal.

Hugs and kisses,
~Em

Subject: Sigh to the third power
From: Mrs.Legolas@kiltnet.com
To: Dru@seattlegrrl.com
Date: 24 January 2004 11:43pm

Dru wrote:
> and I think that was really noble of you, Em. To give up
> a hunky guy just because you weren't madly in love with
> him—well, that just takes balls, grrl. OMC! Balls! Haha-
> hahahah! Anyway, I think you did the right thing. And
> you never know, maybe you'll meet someone else while
> you're there, maybe one of those guys in kilts you're al-
> ways going on about, although I have to say, I don't really
> see what's so hot about them. Not unless they're from
> *Highlander*. Num!

You just have to trust me on this, Dru. When you're stand-ing around in Scotland, guys in kilts are v. hot.

I just wanted to let you know that Devon and Fang are

159

here (yay!), and I was right—they didn't want any haggis either, although both of them had just a little tiny taste because Alec made such a big deal about it being a tradition and all. I'm starting to think that maybe Alec isn't deserving of the hottie-older-man title.

Anyhoodles, Holly gave Ruaraidh the sweater she knitted for him.

"What's this?" he asked, winking at me, which made me feel all weird, because I knew full well he knew that we were knitting sweaters for him. "For me? I thought you were knitting this for yourself!"

Holly blushed and got all girly and stammered out that she thought he'd like it.

"It's very nice, thank you," he said, and kissed her on the cheek, which almost made her faint dead away. I had to pinch her arm so she would remember to breathe. "And what's that you have, Emily?"

OK, now here's the thing: my sweater didn't . . . um . . . quite turn out. It definitely doesn't look like Holly's. For one thing, somehow the back part of it got crooked. And there's the problem with the sleeves, and the holes and curled parts and stuff, so in the end I decided that it was too embarrassing to give it to him. Not just because I didn't want him anymore, but because Holly's sweater looked so much more like a sweater, where my sweater looked like . . . um . . . have you ever seen a tea cozy? Old ladies use them on their teapots to keep them warm. Anyway, my sweater kind of looked like a jumbo tea cozy. So when Ruaraidh asked me what was going on with it, I tried to play it very coolio.

"Oh, this? It's my sweater," I said, pulling it on over my sweatshirt. I gave him what Brother calls my pugnacious look, and dared him to say anything mean about it. "Nice color, huh?"

He eyed it. "Very nice."

"I think it's lovely, Em, just lovely."

I smiled at Holly, and shot Ruaraidh a look that let him know I knew what he was thinking, and he was all wrong. Then he and Holly went out to do something with the lambs. While I was waiting for Devon and Fang to arrive, I went in to see Aunt Tim.

"I'm worried about Holly," I said. Aunt Tim pushed aside the comforter she had draped over her, and peered out at me, her eyes all watery.

"Is she sick again?"

"No," I said with a sigh, and sat on the end of the couch. "She's in love with Ruaraidh."

"Ah," Aunt Tim said. Just "ah."

"Is that all you're going to say? I thought you ancient ones liked to dole out advice and stuff about our love lives. Brother never misses a chance to lecture me."

Aunt Tim started to laugh, but ended up coughing. "I'm sorry, Emily, but I can't think of anything to lecture you on."

I played with the edge of the comforter. "Well . . . maybe you can give me some advice, then."

Her eyebrows went up at that. "If you like. I take it you're not happy that Holly is in love with Ruaraidh? Did you fancy him yourself?"

"Not really. Well, maybe at first, just a little. But I changed my mind the other night. I have a lot of experience with guys, you know, and I can tell when one's not right for me," I told her.

"You can?" Her eyebrows went up even higher. "Tell me

about what happened the other night. Did Ruaraidh kiss you?"

"No, I thought he was going to, which was good because I would have won the contest, but then it turned out he didn't want to."

"Yes, there is the contest, isn't there?"

I gave her a frowny look. "How do you know about that?"

"I saw the chart."

"Geez, does everyone in this house just march into my bedroom when they feel like it?"

She gave me a mom look. For someone who doesn't have kids, she sure had that down pat. Maybe the mom look is something that happens to you when you get old? "I was taking in the laundry that I'd asked you three times to put away."

"Oh. Sorry."

She sneezed five times, then frowned as she mopped up afterward. "Maybe I should have Alec talk to Ruaraidh. . . ."

"About what? He didn't do anything wrong, even if he is kind of an Aidan-lite."

"Aidan?"

"My last boyfriend. He's a poophead. Anyway, what I want to talk to you about isn't me; it's Holly. What do you think I should do about her?"

"About her being in love with Ruaraidh? Why do you have to do anything?"

"Because he's all wrong for her. Let's look at the facts: a) he touched my butt while we were tangoing, b) he thought she was too young until I told him that she had all sorts of boyfriends, and c) he's not madly in love with Holly. A and B wouldn't matter at all if C were false, but it's obvious that he's just using her because now he thinks other guys thinks she's hot, and you know how guys are—they use girls."

"Do they?"

I nodded. "I know; I was used. I'm not saying that Ruaraidh is absolutely a poophead like Aidan, because he doesn't seem as . . . creepy as Aidan, but I definitely think that Holly is more in love with him than he is with her. If he is at all. So the question is, what do I do to make her see that? In a way that won't hurt her. And did I do the right thing telling him that she was mature and stuff? What if he hurts her? What if he treats her like Aidan treated me?"

Aunt Tim pulled a hand out from under the blanket and patted my knee. "Maybe you shouldn't do anything, Em. Maybe you should just let her be, and not try to direct her life."

I twisted the cord on the edge of the comforter cover. "But if I don't do something, she'll end up devastated when she finds out that Ruaraidh doesn't love her. I like her, Aunt Tim! She's my only GF here in England. She's different than me; she's a lot more sensitive. She doesn't talk about stuff like what she's feeling, but I know that her life will be over if she agrees to be Ruaraidh's girlfriend and then he acts like a poop to her."

"You don't know what he feels about her. Emily, I commend your desire to save Holly from heartache, but don't you think that she has a right to live her own life and make her own mistakes?"

"That's stupid. Why should she make mistakes when I can stop her from doing them?"

She smiled and cuddled back under the blankies. "Let me put it this way—when you were dating Aidan, would you have wanted someone to stop you early in the relationship and tell you he was all wrong for you?"

I thought about that for a few minutes. "It would have been nice if someone had told me he was a poophead."

She did the eyebrow-raising thing again.

"Oh, OK, I probably wouldn't have listened," I said as I stood up to go upstairs and change for the guys. "All right, I won't save Holly from certain disaster, but if she dies of a broken heart, you're going to have to explain to her parents that the only reason I didn't stop it is because you said I shouldn't."

"Deal. Oh, Emily?"

I paused at the door to the sitting room and looked back.

She smiled. "I think you're a wonderful friend. I wish I had had a friend who cared as much about me when I was your age."

I did the shoulder-twitch thing that you do when someone says something nice and it makes you want to puddle up, but you don't want them to see that, yet you still want them to know that you appreciate what they said, then trotted upstairs to get ready for Devon and Fang.

Oh, shoot, I have to go. There's a big windstorm, and Aunt Tim says I shouldn't be on the computer in case the power goes out. I'll e-mail you the rest as soon as I can.

Be sure to tell me how the *ROTK* date with Tim went!

Hugs and kissies,
~Em

Subject: I'm back, where are you?
From: Mrs.Legolas@kiltnet.com
To: Dru@seattlegrrl.com
Date: 26 January 2004 10:02am

All right, it's been a whole day and a half since I wrote you; why haven't you e-mailed me? Are you OK? Has something happened that you're afraid to tell me? How was your date on Friday? Meh, Dru! You can't do this to me; you know how worried I get when you don't e-mail me at least five times a day!

Well, I'm going to assume that you're not just being spazzy and that something has happened to keep you from e-mailing me, but if I find out you're deliberately withholding e-mail, I'm going to be so pissed! Although now I'm worried about what's happened to you.

I couldn't e-mail you yesterday because it was still windy in the morning, with the power browning out and stuff, and then by lunchtime we were gone, and we didn't get back until around midnight last night. It was a really long day. I've got a ton to tell you, but I have to do it in order or else it won't make sense.

Let's see, where did I leave off? Oh, yeah, when Devon and Fang came up. Nothing much happened that night except I was really, really happy to see them. Fang looked just the same as he did the last time I saw him, except he's letting his hair grow out a little, which is good because it's curly and stuff, and I like guys with longish dark hair. And he's got those nummy puppy-dog eyes. Devon . . . oh, Dru, Devon is . . . hoo, baby! He just got his hair redone, so the blond tips looked really cool on his black hair. And of course he's got those fabu blue eyes with the long, long eyelashes.

Question of the day: Why is it guys always get long eyelashes? It's not like they use them or anything. I think it's unfair that they should get long lashes while we get short, stubby ones.

Anyway, both guys looked great, and they were happy to see Holly and me, and I was v. happy to see them, and we played Twister after dinner, except Holly was too shy to play, so she sat next to Ruaraidh and looked at him a lot. I just wish I could tell her . . . But no, I've made a promise to myself that I won't. I don't know how adults do this letting-kids-make-their-own mistakes stuff. It's so frustrating when I can see that he's *all wrong* for her!

Yesterday we left after breakfast and went to Inverness, which is an OK town—it has two malls, although they call them *shopping centres* here—and, of course, went shopping. I had Aunt Tim's early birthday money, and the tiny bit I scrounged off of the 'rents, so we had fun looking in all the shops and seeing what kids up here wear.

"Hey, look, a Starbucks!" I said, pointing. "Coolio! Let's go get lattes!"

Fang groaned (he doesn't like coffee). "We've been here for more than three hours; I could stand something a little stronger than coffee."

"Me, too," Devon said, and took my hand. He kissed my knuckles (isn't he dreamy?) and grinned at me. "As much as I love spending hours wandering through shops while you look at every single item available for sale, I think Fang and I need a little reward for our good behavior. A reward of the liquid kind, if ya ken."

"Coffee is liquid," I said, my insides doing a girly thing at his grin and his fake Scottish accent. "Maybe Holly would like—Holly? Hey! Where'd she go?"

Fang rubbed his nose and followed when Devon pushed me out of the store we were in—the Gap—yes, they have them here, too. "She went off with that Ruaraidh bloke."

"Where?" I asked as we wandered down the middle of the mall. "I'm not sure she should be left alone with him."

"Oh?" Devon, who was still holding my hand, stopped to look at me. He glanced at Fang. Fang didn't say anything, just watched me. "Maybe *you'd* rather be alone with him?"

"Me?" I looked from Devon to Fang. I thought at first they might be joking, but they both looked serious. "No, I don't want him."

"Don't you, now," Devon said, smiling again. "I find that very interesting. Don't you find that interesting, Fang?"

Fang just looked at Devon's thumb where it was rubbing over my fingers. "Yes, very interesting."

"Do you plan on doing anything about it?"

Fang glanced at me for a second, then looked away as he put his hands in his pockets. "You know I said I was going to wait."

"Um . . ." Something was going on between them, but I didn't know what. It was like they were doing some guy-speak or something that wasn't understandable to females. "What are you waiting for, Fang?"

Devon kept his eyes on Fang. "I don't have any such noble intentions, mate."

Fang shrugged, then started walking away.

"What are you guys talking about?" I asked, watching Fang go off on his own. I don't know why, but I felt like he was disappointed in me somehow, which is stupid, because I didn't even know what it was they were talking about! "Why is Fang leaving? Did I say something?"

"He's just going to get you a latte," Devon said, watching me closely. "See?"

Fang went into the Starbucks.

"Oh. That's awfully sweet of him."

"He's my best mate. So you don't fancy this Ruaraidh bloke at all, then?"

I blinked and crossed my fingers. And before you say I was lying, I wasn't. I had drooled over the thought of Ruaraidh, but didn't anymore. And Devon wasn't asking if I had ever wanted him; he was asking about now. And I didn't. Want Ruaraidh now, that is. I mean, he was still v. hot and all, but I didn't want him. Not that way. "Um. No, I don't fancy him."

Devon smiled and squeezed my hand, pulling me toward a courtyard area with a bunch of white chairs and tables. "Think you could fancy me?"

OHMICROD! I stared at him for a few seconds before I realized my mouth was hanging open and I was probably drooling all over the place. "Wha—what?"

"I said"—he pulled out a white metal chair for me. I sat— "do you think you could fancy me?"

Now this is the scary thing, Dru. My brain kind of ran around in my head the way your hamster Teddy did when he ate one of your mom's diet pills. Was Devon asking me to be his GF, or was he just wondering if I liked him enough to be his GF, or was he asking me for some other reason that I couldn't possibly imagine because I had a hamster brain that couldn't think straight?

"Um. Well . . . yeah. I could . . . um . . . fancy you."

"Good," he said, and brushed a strand of hair off my cheek, tucking it behind my ear. I just about melted into a great big puddle at the touch, and it was just one finger! "There's Holly."

"Huh?" I tried to make the hamster calm down, but even after Holly and Ruaraidh sat down (holding hands, and her with a bright, shiny, happy look on her face), and Fang brought me a latte, I still couldn't figure out what happened.

"I'm so happy," Holly said a little bit later, when we made a dash to the ladies' room before we went off to the Circus of the Darned. "I feel like I'm going to explode, I'm so happy. Oh, Em! He's so wonderful! He kissed me! Twice! I hope you don't mind that I won the contest. You don't mind, do you? I didn't think you'd mind because you've got Fang and Devon, and it's obvious what's going on there, and I'm happy for you too, because even though you said you weren't going to have a boyfriend for six months, I know you were kind of wishing you had one, and now we both have them, and isn't life wonderful? I'm so glad you talked me into coming up here. I'd have died if I had to live my life without meeting Ruaraidh!"

I stared at Holly. She was gushing, and she's never gushed before, not the whole time I've known her. She never says much, and now she was gushing! I don't gush when I'm madly in love with a guy, do I? Sheesh, I hope I don't. You'd tell me if I did, wouldn't you?

After I got over the shock of Holly gushing, I started thinking about what she said. The kissing-Ruaraidh bit was no surprise; it was a foregone conclusion (as Brother always says). But the bit about me wanting a BF, and the "obvious what's going" on bit (which must mean that Devon really is going to ask me to be his GF), well, that was a surprise. "Uh . . . first of all, no, I don't mind that you've won the contest. I'm happy if you're happy that Ruaraidh kissed you."

"Oh, I am. I'm very happy. Very, very, very happy!" She spun around in a circle, which was a bit embarrassing, since everyone in the bathroom stared at us. I grabbed her arm and pushed her into one of the stalls, closing the door behind us. "Emily, what are you doing?"

I frowned at her as she stared in horror at the toilet. "Oh, for Pete's sake, it's just a toilet; it's not going to give you rabies or anything. You don't have to sit on it; I just want to talk to you about . . . uh . . ." I stopped because I had promised myself I wouldn't interfere by warning her about Ruaraidh.

"About *your* boyfriend?" she asked with a coy little smile.

I sighed. It was no use; I couldn't do it. I decided I'd tackle the other issue. "I don't know what to say, Holly. You know I've always been open to having a BF if one came along who wasn't a poophead like Aidan, and you know how much I've always liked Devon, but I have to admit that I was v. surprised when he asked me if I could fancy him."

Her smile faded. "Devon?" she asked, blinking really quickly.

"I know; it's never a good idea to date a friend, because then if the dating thing turns out icky, you've lost a friend as well as a boyfriend, and I have to admit that although I've always thought Devon was majorly *über*-coolio and hot and all, I never thought I'd have a chance with him, because he always has a ton of girls hanging off of him. And he's so flirty! It's fun when he's not your BF, but I'm not sure I want a BF who's so flirty with every girl he meets. And I have to be honest, because you're my friend and I know you won't tell anyone, but he hasn't actually asked me to be his girlfriend yet; he just asked me if I fancied him, and when I said I could, he said good."

Eeek! I just did a word count. Holly's gush was a hundred and nineteen words, while my answer to her question above was a hundred and forty! OHMICROD! I'm a gusher! *Meh!*

She blinked a bit more, then said, "Oh. Well . . . oh. That sounds . . . good."

"You don't think he's just teasing me or something, do you?" I asked, worried a bit by her confused look.

"No, I'm sure he's not. Erm . . . why don't we talk about this later? I know Ruaraidh was really looking forward to seeing the Circus of the Darned." She blushed and looked down at her fingers, her lips doing a half-smile thing. "He said there's a tattoo booth there, and that I could pick out a tattoo for him."

I had a teeny, tiny pang of jealousy over that. No guy has ever offered to let me pick out a tat for him. Devon already had one, a really cool dragon that wrapped around his upper arm, so he probably wouldn't want another one.

Anyhoodles, we all crammed into Devon's car and headed off to the place just outside of town where the circus was set up. I sat in the back with Holly and Ruaraidh because Fang looked kind of sad, and I thought he might not want to sit with them. You know how it is if you're the only one not with someone when you're out with a bunch of people. Not that I was with Devon, but I *might* be. Oh, you know what I mean.

The Circus of the Darned was the *über*est of all *über*coolio shows! It really was more of a sideshow, you know, the kind that has freaks and stuff? Only these people didn't have flippers for hands or anything icky like that. They were great! They put on a show with music and singing and stuff, with four guys and two girls. There was a woman who did a dance with power tools, and a guy in a bondage outfit who did stuff on a bed of nails (and they were real, because you could see the marks on his back), and a contortionist who balanced on a tower of beer cans and twisted himself into a big knot, and another guy who lifted stuff with his tongue and—major ew!—with his nipples. Or rather, the rings in his nipples.

"That's something, isn't it?" Devon whispered in my ear. I was sitting between him and Fang on the bench. Holly and Ruaraidh were behind us somewhere (I was a bit worried about her, but when I asked Fang earlier if we shouldn't sit with them, he got a really sad look on his face and said, "Sometimes you just have to let people do what they want to do." Doesn't that break your heart? Poor Fang. He really needs a girlfriend). Devon's arm rubbed mine. "Can't say that my nipples are up to lifting a rubbish bin."

"Yeah, well, you don't have the hardware that Nipple Boy has," I answered, and tried not to feel all gushy because he was whispering right next to my ear, *and* touching my arm. I got a bit panicky for a moment that he was going to ask me to be his girlfriend right there in the middle of the Darned acts, but he didn't, so I relaxed again.

"You like those nipple rings, do you?" he asked, his mouth gently touching my ear. It gave me the shivers, which went into shiver overtime when he traced a finger down my arm, then started rubbing little circles on the back of my hand.

I stared at the back of my hand where his fingers were stroking it. It didn't look sexy at all; it just looked like the back of a (still slightly orange) hand, but it felt so sexy!

"I used to," I whispered back, without turning to look at him, because I was just sure if I did, he'd kiss me, and I didn't want everyone sitting around us to see us kissing, because it's, like, you know, *so personal!* "But I decided last year that I didn't like them."

"Why?" The word was soft and warm in my ear, and sent even more shivers down my neck and arms. His fingers slid underneath the wrist of my sweater and started stroking a path up my arm. My arm! It was like his fingers were on fire or something, because I went tingly all over, and the little hairs on the back of my neck stood on end, and the nipple thing was happening (couldn't you just die when they do that?), and all of a sudden I felt really flushed, like I was blushing.

I had to swallow twice before I could talk. "Well, I saw this guy get one of his rings caught in his shirt when he was taking it off at the beach, and it ripped his nipple off, and it was really gross, and ever since then I can't see them without remembering that guy screaming and running around bleeding and everyone digging through the sand trying to find his nipple so they could sew it back on. They never did. I heard from a friend that he was going to get a nipple transplant, but that it would cost too much, and his parents wouldn't pay for it, so he had to go around with one normal nipple and a nipple stump, which just sounds really gross, don't you think?"

Devon made the snorty-nose noise you make when you're trying not to laugh out loud. His fingers slid back down to my wrist, and he squeezed my hand. "Emily, you are without a doubt the most unique girl I've ever known."

"Oh." I didn't know what that meant. Unique good or unique bad? I figured I'd better just ask. "Um. Do you like unique girls?"

His thumb curled under to rub my palm. I almost shot up off the bench, it was such an . . . intimate touch! I know, I know, it's just the palm, but you sit in the dark with a really hottalicious guy friend who you think might want you as a GF, and you let him rub his thumb over your palm, and then you'll see!

"As a matter of fact, I do."

Whew! It was good unique after all. "Do you think . . . uh . . . you could fancy a unique girl?"

"Definitely."

OMC! I sat there wanting to dance and sing and yell and jump around and basically act just like Holly did, but instead I had to maintain the fabled Emily cool, so I didn't say anything as we watched the next act (two guys holding roses in their mouths, which were snapped out of their mouth by the two girls with big bullwhips).

But I did lean into Devon just a little bit when he slid his arm around my back. I didn't want to lean into him too much, because Fang was on my other side, and he was sad enough because everyone was taken but him, but I did lean a little bit, which was v. cool.

The final act was awesome! Two sword swallowers came out with a double sword (they welded two swords together by the handle parts) and said they were going to do a double sword swallow.

"Do you think those blades are real?" Fang leaned toward me to ask. Just as he did, the guys onstage slashed the blades through a couple of oranges.

"I guess they are," I answered. "How do they do that? Swallow swords, I mean?"

"They relax the muscles in their throat," Devon said. "I knew a bloke at one of the Ren Faires Mum was always dragging me to who was a swallower."

The power-tool girl tied a rope around one of the guy's

legs (giving him a big snog when she was done); then he was hauled upside down into the air until he hung over a small barrel. Power-tool Girl handed him the sword, and he slowly swallowed half of it. Then the second guy climbed the barrel and started swallowing the bottom half of the sword from underneath, while Guy #1 was lowered slowly until Guy #2 swallowed his half of the sword. I have to say, it was totally, totally cool! Power-tool Girl came in with a big noisy tool, and while the two guys were filled up with sword, cut the sword in half!

Wow just doesn't cut it. Cut! Hahahahah!

After that we wandered around and looked at some of the attractions. Devon didn't try to hold my hand, which at first made me worried, but then I figured out that he was aware that Fang wasn't too happy, and he must have felt (like I did) that it wouldn't be nice at all to act all happy in front of him. Holly went off with Ruaraidh before I could say anything to her (not that I knew what I was going to say), so Devon and Fang and I went to look at the sideshow stuff.

"What do you want to see first?" Fang asked, looking at the board listing attractions. "There's a palm reader, and a tattoo artist, an aura photographer, and Mr. Parker's Museum of Oddities."

"How about the palm reader first, then the oddities; then we'll have our aura pictures taken?"

"You're the boss," Devon said, and gave me a grin that made my knees melt. We saw Madame Zelda (who didn't look very Zelda-ish), paid over our five pounds ("My treat," Devon said, which was awfully nice of him because I knew that Fang was really broke right then because he'd lost his job at the stable), and had our palms read. Fang's reading was pretty good (he liked animals, had a studious nature, and would love only one woman in his lifetime), and Devon's was even better (she predicted that he'd be successful in love and business—which is spot on, because you know that he's already the most popular guy in Piddlesville, and I'm sure he'll be a great engineer, too—and that he'd have three children—*I* plan on having three children! Coincidence or fate?), but the best, the really hair-standing-on-end, creepily wonderful best was my reading.

I went last because I wanted to see what sort of things she was going to say. If she was going to do embarrassing stuff like that woman we saw at Disney World who told me that I was going to have trouble in my woman parts if I didn't watch out, then I wasn't going to have my palm read. But she didn't say anything like that; she just looked at my hand, her fingers tracing the lines. "You have a very warm heart, but it is divided at the moment between concern for one who is close to you, and a new love interest."

See what I mean? *Totally freaky!*

"You are far from home, but you have farther to go before you reach your journey's end."

Now this is where it gets really weird. You remember I told you the parentals were thinking about letting me to go Paris during spring break to do one of those weeklong intensive French classes? Well, this morning Brother called up to say when they were going to be in Edinburgh tomorrow to pick us up, and he said that he and Mom talked about it, and they decided that since I'd done such a good job here, they were going to let me go! Yay!

Oh, geez, I just got goose bumps thinking about how weird it is that Zelda knew it even before I did.

"Your heart line is strong and unbroken. You, too, will have one mate, a man whom fate has chosen to be your companion in this life, and all the lives that follow."

I peeked at Devon out of the corner of my eye. He was talking quietly to Fang, his head turned away from me. Was Devon my one true love?

"But before you find him"—I turned back to Zelda, who was looking at the side of my hand—"you will have many trials to overcome, many lessons to learn."

I sighed. Why was there always a catch to everything? Still, she got the lessons stuff right. You don't become a Nobel prize–winning physicist just by your good looks.

"You are brave of heart and strong of spirit. You follow your heart rather than your head. You should follow your instincts rather than relying upon opinions of those around you. You will not be happy or successful unless you take charge of your life and make it what you want."

I liked that! She said a few things about me having a major illness when I was older, but that I'd come out of it stronger than before, and then it was over. As we left Zelda's tent, Holly hurried up to me, hauling Ruaraidh by his hand.

"There you are! I've been looking for you everywhere. Have you seen the oddities?"

"No, are they good?" I asked. Devon came up next to me and rubbed his knuckles against my hip.

He is *so* hot!

Holly dropped Ruaraidh's hand and, grabbing my arm, started to drag me off toward the Mr. Parker's Museum of Oddities tent. Holly! Shy little Holly! She's never dragged me *anywhere*! "Boy, you get a BF and you go all Buffy on me. Holly, you're hurting my wrist. What are you doing?"

"You have to see it; it's . . . it's . . . Oh, I don't even know how to explain it; you just have to see it."

I looked back toward the guys, but Ruaraidh was looking at the tattoo tent. Devon and Fang were still talking together, looking at the tat picture boards outside of the tent. Devon stopped long enough to wave a hand at us and yell, "Go on; we'll be along in a few."

"All right, what's so important that you've got to take me away from Devon? He's about to ask me to be his girlfriend, I just know it! And maybe he'll let me pick out a tat for him."

"This is what's important," she said, and let go of my wrist so she could push me into the tent. "I can't stand it, Emily. It's awful. You have to do something. I can't stand to see the poor little thing suffer."

The Museum of Oddities was a bunch of cubicle-like areas separated by long blue curtains hung on an iron framework, making a whole bunch of little rooms all inside the one tent. The first room we came to had a sign pinned on the curtain that said *Oddities of the Animal World*.

"I don't see what's so horrible about this," I said, glancing at a display case that had a bunch of stuffed animals sitting around a tea table. Kind of a teddy bear's picnic, except these were kitties and squirrels and stuff. I was about to say something else to Holly when I looked back at the case, stepping closer and bending down so I could see in it. "*Oh, my God!* Those aren't stuffed animals, they're . . . *stuffed animals*!"

Holly stood beside me, doing that wringing-the-hands thing. "It's not that; look over there. That's what I want you to see."

I stared at the display, my whole body getting ready to start screaming. The first scene in the case was of kittens—real live kittens, or real dead kittens, kittens that had been alive and were now dead and stuffed—sitting around a small round table that had doll's cups and saucers and little cakes and a teapot and stuff. The kittens were wearing little dresses and hats and OHMICROD they were dead kittens! "This is awful! It's got to be illegal or something!"

"Over here, look over here!" Holly said, just about dancing behind me. I looked in the second half of the case. There were two squirrels in little smoking jackets with those red fez hats, smoking pipes.

"Jeezumcrow, who did this? They ought to go to jail!"

"Please, Emily, I can't stand its poor little eyes!"

"Just a sec, I have to see . . . Oh, my God, look at that! It's a marching band made up of mice! That's just sick! And what are those? Guinea pigs? Are they playing cricket? Whoever did this is a monster, a certifiable monster!"

"Emily, please!"

I looked in the next case and screamed. "Will you look at what they did to the poor little innocent bunnies? This is terrible! I'm going to complain! All those poor little dead bunnies dressed up like Victorian schoolkids . . . It's just repulsive, that's what it is. This isn't an oddity; it's a blight upon human . . . um . . . existence! Yeah, that's it; it's a blight!"

"Emily Williams!" I looked up at Holly, surprised she could yell that loud. We weren't the only ones in the museum, but we were the only people in the animal area.

"What?"

She pointed at a small terrarium-type cage, the kind you had when you owned the lizards. The bottom of it was filled with grass and little shrubby things, and dirt mounded into what looked like a tiny cave. It didn't look at all nice, like someone hadn't cleaned it in a long time. It smelled awful.

179

"Tristan," she said.

"Tristan?"

"Tristan!"

I walked over to look. I figured nothing could be worse than dead little bunnies and kitties dressed up in clothes and posed in cute little scenes.

I was *so* wrong.

I stared at Tristan for a few seconds, my mouth hanging *wide* open. "My . . . God! Is that . . . Does that have . . . Am I seeing it . . ."

Holly nodded, her lip quivery as her eyes got all puddly looking at it. "Look at its poor little eyes, Emily. It's suffering."

I looked at its little eyes . . . and its little eyes. I looked back and forth. I couldn't believe what I was seeing, and was just about to tell her it was fake when one set of the eyes blinked, and the head moved.

The left head.

Tristan the Two-headed Hedgehog, the sign over the cage read.

"What're we going to do?" Holly asked, her fingers curled through the metal framework holding the lid on the cage.

"Do? Well . . . uh . . . we can complain to someone."

"It's suffering! It doesn't want to be in a dirty little cage, stared at by thousands of people just like it was a freak; it wants to be free. Can't you see that?"

"Yeah, OK, but I don't know what we can do."

"You can *do* something," Holly said, giving me one of her "you can do anything" looks. "You tell me what to do, and I'll help. I can't stand seeing Tristan suffer like that."

"Yeah, but it's just a hedgehog . . . and a half."

Holly's fingers stroked down the front side of the glass near one of Tristan's heads. "I never told you this, but I had a pet hedgehog when I was a little girl. Her name was Emily."

I stared at her in surprise. "No!"

She nodded. "That's why I liked you right away; you reminded me of my Emily. She died a couple of years ago. I'm . . . I'm still not over it."

"Really?" I felt my eyes go a bit misty. You know how I am about animals. I still miss Pot Pie. He was the best dog ever. I looked back at Tristan. "Well . . ."

"Oh, I knew you didn't have a cruel heart," Holly said, all happy again. "I knew you'd do something. What's your plan?"

"Plan? Uh . . ." Tristan's right head turned to look at me, just like it heard her, its beady little black eyes glistening like it was going to cry. I swear to you, Dru, it was trying to tell me something. In that moment, something happened inside of me, something important. I knew that just like Zelda said, I had to take my life in my own hands and make things happen. "Fang."

"Fang?"

"We'll take it to Fang. He's a vet student; he'll know whether or not Tristan is suffering, and if he is, he can make him better. If he's not, Fang will know what he needs to eat and stuff, and then we can set him free."

"Yes!" Holly said, doing an excited little dance.

"You go watch at the door for people," I said as I peeled off my coat. I pulled the lid off of the cage and climbed onto a box that stood behind Tristan's glass house.

"Be careful of his spines," Holly whispered loudly.

Tristan didn't do anything until just before I was about to

scoop him up in my coat, and then he made a funny little squealing noise out of one of his mouths.

"Shhh!" I told him, and bundled him up carefully in my jacket. "Let's get out of here!"

Holly raced out ahead of me, spinning around at the end of the corridor to gesture wildly at me. "People! I think it's Mr. Parker!"

"Crap! Um . . ." I looked around, but the museum tent was like a maze with all the blue curtained-off sections. I chewed my lip for a second, trying to think of something as I held the squirming Tristan firmly, but not so firmly that I hurt him. He squealed again.

"Do something!" Holly said, peeking around the corner. "They're coming!"

I looked around us, but there was nowhere to hide, so I did the only thing I could do: I stuffed Tristan and my coat under my sweater. "Do I look pregnant?" I asked Holly, whose eyes were just about bugging out at me.

"Er—"

"Here," I said, trying to mold Tristan and my coat under my sweater until they looked round and not all pointy and pokey-outy, like I had a two-headed hedgehog shoved under my sweater.

"Er—"

"Walk in front of me," I ordered, and scooted up close behind her as we headed for the exit. "Maybe they won't notice."

There were a group of people standing at the entrance of the tent, where a guy in an old-time bowler hat and bow tie was handing out pamphlets and talking about the displays. Holly and I tried to slip past them, but Tristan was making shrill little yipping noises, and even though Holly started coughing loudly to cover up the noise, evidently Mr. Parker (if that's who he was) noticed my stomach moving under my sweater, because he stopped talking to the people and turned to yell at us as we hurried out the exit. "Oy! You! What do you have under your jumper?"

"Run!" I yelled at Holly, pulling the squirming Tristan-in-coat package out from under my sweater as I took off at warp five. We raced through the crowd, Mr. Parker yelling stuff about someone stopping us, that we had stolen something, yadda yadda yadda. We dodged around clumps of people wandering around the circus, everyone stopping to stare at us as we ran like the wind.

"Maybe we should split up?" Holly asked as we spun around a corner, racing past the concession stands.

"Fang," I said, panting (yeah, yeah, so I'm out of shape, so what? I had just liberated a two-headed hedgehog! Give me a break!). "What we need is Fang. He'll know what to do."

Just as I said the last word, Fang, Devon, and Ruaraidh strolled out from the main aisle toward us. Holly started yelling at Ruaraidh to help us, waving her hands around in the air. I clutched the squirming hedgehog tighter (which made him squeal even louder—I think both heads were squealing, to tell the truth), and threw myself toward the guys, not even thinking about the horrible stitch that was pulling my side. The guys all stopped and looked at us like we were . . . well, like we were a two-headed hedgehog.

Holly, who was faster than me (she wasn't hauling Tristan around), ran up to Ruaraidh and threw herself into his arms. I ran toward Fang, then decided that right there in the middle of the circus with a pissed-off Mr. Parker yelling behind us probably wasn't the best place to explain the whole Tristan thing, so I just yelled, "Tristan," as I raced around them, down the last line of tents to where the cars were parked.

"Tristan?" Ruaraidh asked.

"We stole him," Holly said.

"Liberated, not stole," I bellowed.

Devon looked at me like I was insane. Fang squinted for a second at the coat in my arms (he said later one of Tristan's snouts was poking through it); then he grabbed Devon by the arm and yelled to follow me.

By the time we made it to the car, I was all in and couldn't talk. "Drive," I said in a gasp as I jumped into the back, pulling Fang in after me.

Devon drove. He burned rubber getting us out of the parking lot.

"What is it?" Ruaraidh asked, turning around in the front seat and trying to see what was wrapped up in my coat. "You stole something? What did you steal?"

"Tristan," Holly answered (he was her BF, after all). "It was horrible, Ruaraidh; you should have seen his eyes. They were so sad!"

"What's a Tristan?" Devon asked, glancing at us in the rearview mirror.

I (still gasping for breath—I really have to get back to jogging every day) peeled back my coat until one of Tristan's heads showed.

"Oh. It's just a hedgehog," Ruaraidh said, turning back around in his seat.

"A hedgehog? I'm risking a speeding ticket for a hedge-hog?"

"It's not just a hedgehog," I corrected Ruaraidh, then peeled back the rest of the coat. Tristan's little eyes blinked in the overhead light that Devon had flipped on.

"It's two hedgehogs. No, it's . . . holy sh*t!" Fang said. (I know you hate that word, so I bleeped it for you) "It has two heads!"

"It's Tristan, the two-headed hedgehog, although really, when you think about it, shouldn't he have two names? I mean, shouldn't each head get a name of its own?" I asked.

"It has two heads," Fang said again, staring at it.

"Yes, I think it should have another name; that only seems right," Holly agreed. "What about Charles? I like the name Charles."

"One head, two heads. One body. Two heads on one body," Fang said, leaning over my lap to look at Tristan/Charles (henceforth known as TC).

"Charles is good. I think the left head looks like a Charles, don't you?" I asked Holly. She leaned forward to look just as Ruaraidh leaned over the seat to look. The two of them clunked heads.

"One hedgehog, two heads."

I punched Fang in the arm (gently). "I think we've all got that now, Fang. The question is, what are you going to do for him?"

"What do you mean, what am I going to do for him?"

I gave him a Look. "You should have seen his filthy cage; it was terrible! Holly thinks Tristan is sick. You're the almost-vet; you have to take care of him and make him better."

Fang looked from me down to TC, then back up to me. "I am?"

I had to punch him on the arm again. "Yes, you are; you take an oath or something, don't you? To help animals in need? Look at him; he's suffered terribly being in that horrible terrarium thing. Not only was it dirty and ucky, but he was obviously being abused."

185

"He was, he truly was," Holly said, her eyes all weepy. "And there were people laughing at him when we went in there earlier. That's very unkind. His poor little eyes were practically begging us to save him."

"Please?" I asked Fang. I let go of TC just long enough to put my hand over Fang's so I could give it a *please* squeeze, but . . . well, TC took that moment to escape.

"*Ack!*" I yelled when he slithered down my leg and dashed under the seat in front of me.

"Ack what?" Devon asked.

"He's loose!"

"What, the two-headed hedgehog? It's loose? In my car?"

"Yes, it's loose. It's under the front seat. Eeek! I think it touched me with one of its heads!"

There was a horrible squeal of tires as Devon slammed on the brakes and pulled over to the side of the road. Luckily there was no one behind us. We were on a road outside of town, next to a big field of cows. All four car doors flew open as the five of us jumped out of the car, running a few feet away, then turning and looking back at the car.

"What were you eeking about?" Devon asked me, bending over so he could peer in under the car seat.

"It touched me! With one of its cold little noses."

"You were holding the bloody thing; why are you so freaked about it touching you?" Ruaraidh asked.

"I had it wrapped in my coat; it wasn't touching me personally!" I rubbed my ankle where I think it touched me.

"Oh, for . . . This is ridiculous. It's just a hedgehog," Devon said, and bravely marched the few feet over to the car and banged on the front seat a couple of times. TC must have squeaked at him, because he jumped back and looked at Fang. "You get it."

"What?"

"Emily's right; you're the vet. You get it."

"I won't be a vet for three more years, and besides, my experience with animals is limited strictly to those bearing only one head each."

"Well, if you don't get him, who will?" I asked, rubbing my arms. "It's cold out here. We can't just stand around here waiting for him to go to sleep."

"You stole it," Ruaraidh said. "You should get it."

"I didn't steal it; I liberated it. There's a difference."

"Not much of one."

"Ha!"

In the end, no one got TC. While we were arguing, he ran out the side door. Holly, who was standing behind the car, saw him jump down onto the side of the road, then race off into the tall grass that ran alongside a ditch.

The rest of the ride home was pretty quiet, Holly leaning on Ruaraidh, crying quietly (she worried about TC surviving in the wild), Fang sitting with his eyes shut, looking tired, and me . . . well, I was trying to figure out if, based on the "definitely" comment Devon made at the circus, whether or not we were BF/GF.

Potty break. BRB.

Subject: What, you're STILL not e-mailing me?
From: Mrs.Legolas@kiltnet.com
To: Dru@seattlegrrl.com
Date: 26 January 2004 10:27am

Oh. Wait. I guess it's only two in the morning there. Never mind. You had just better e-mail me the minute you get up!

So where was I? Um . . . oh, yeah, after the circus. When we got home Ruaraidh wanted to check on his dogs, so he headed off to the barn while the rest of us went into the house. Alec was in the kitchen warming up some soup for Aunt Tim.

"Did you have a nice time?" he asked as we all trooped in.

"Yeah, it was great. Well, except Tristan/Charles pooped on my coat. I'm going to go throw it in the washer."

"Tristan/Charles?" Alec asked, holding a mug of soup.

"The two-headed hedgehog Emily and Holly stole."

"Liberated," I yelled from the laundry room.

"They—"

"Liberated!"

"—a two-headed hedgehog?"

"It's all right; Fang looked it over," Devon said. "It was healthy, so I'm sure it won't infect any of the area hedgehogs. Right, Fang?"

"Well, I didn't really get a chance to *examine* it. . . ."

"It escaped," Holly said, obviously still a bit teary-eyed. I could hear her sniffle from the laundry room. "It just ran out into the darkness of the night, alone, all alone, with no one to help it if one of its heads gets stuck in something. All . . . by . . . itself."

"If it was well enough to poop on my coat, it was well enough to survive on its own," I said, coming back into the room. "Oh, Holly, don't. He'll be all right; I'm sure he will."

It took us fifteen minutes to get Holly calmed down enough so she'd go to bed. Aunt Tim was already in bed, and Alec—after shaking his head and saying that if he didn't know anything about a hedgehog liberation, he couldn't be held as an accessory after the fact—went upstairs to bed.

Fang rubbed a hand through his hair, gave me an odd look (I had absolutely *no* idea what it meant), then gathered up the pillows and blankets and sheets Aunt Tim had left out for the guys to sleep on the couches in the sitting room and TV room, and toddled off to his couch.

I looked at Devon. He looked at me. He was sitting on the kitchen table, watching me. I must have been more tired than I thought, because rather than being *über*-cool and stuff, I blurted out, "Are you going to kiss me?"

"Depends. Do you want me to?"

I thought about it for a few seconds. I think something was wrong with my brain, because instead of thinking things and waiting for them to be approved for speaking, my mouth started saying stuff without first getting the OK from Mr. Brain. "I like you, Devon. I like you a lot as a friend. You're funny and flirty and sooooo scrumdillyicious, but you can like someone a lot and not want them to be your BF."

He blinked at me.

"Oh, who'm I fooling? Of course I want you to kiss me. This means you're my boyfriend, right? I mean, it's serious?"

He reached into his back pocket, then pulled out a little box and gave it to me.

"What is it?" I asked, looking at the little black box.

"Open it."

I opened it. Inside, on pretty white satin, was a gold claddagh ring (you know, the kind with the two hands holding the heart), with tiny little green stones on either side of the heart. I stared at it for a minute, then looked up at him. "Oh, my Crod! Is this an engagement ring?"

He laughed and grabbed one of my hands, pulling me close until I stood between his knees. "No, it's just a friendship ring. I thought you'd like it."

"I do like it! I love it. It's beautiful. I like it better than any other ring I have, except my Grandma Teuke's garnet, and I love that the most because she gave it to me right before she died."

He laughed again and took the box, sliding the ring onto my ring finger. "Hmm. Not a bad fit. How does it feel?"

"Fine," I said, my heart doing a bunch of thumpy things as he slid his hands up my arms to the back of my neck. He just looked at me for a minute, and I wondered if I was supposed to do something. Maybe I should have had something for him? "Are you going to kiss me now?"

"Yes, I'm going to kiss you now. I've waited a long time for this, Emily."

"You have?" I asked, kind of whispery against his lips, because the whole time he was talking, he was pulling me closer to him until I leaned up against him. His legs tightened next to me as he kissed around the corners of my mouth in tiny little feathery kisses. All my insides went quivery.

"I have. I've wanted to kiss you since that first day I saw you."

"You did?" I asked, feeling like a moron, but I honestly think my brain had stopped working at that point, because it wasn't offering any suggestions of anything to say.

"I did, but you wanted Aidan, so I waited. But now you're my girl, aren't you?"

"Um," I said, and all of a sudden my brain kicked in.

"Um?" he asked, kissing along my jaw over to my ear.

"Yeah."

He stopped kissing me to look at me. "Um what?"

"Well . . . every time I've seen you, well, almost every time, you've always had girls with you."

"I like girls," he said, giving me that wonderfully devilish grin that made my stomach turn somersaults.

"I know. That's . . . uh . . . well, that's the problem. I didn't like it when Aidan . . . you know. With other girls. I want a boyfriend who's all mine, one who thinks I'm important."

Devon made kind of a strange half smile, his finger tracing a line from my ear to my jaw. It tickled, but I didn't want him to stop. "You want a lot out of a relationship, don't you?"

"Yeah," I said, and sighed. "I'm sorry, but that's just the way I am."

"OK," he said.

It was my turn to blink. "OK? You mean . . . OK? You still want me, even though you can't date any other girls?"

He smiled, then slid both hands around so he was cupping my face, and kissed the tip of my nose. "OK, I want you and I won't date any other girls. Good enough?"

I smiled. I was a bit too shy to kiss him, but I leaned my cheek into his hand until his lips did a little baby kiss on mine. "Good enough."

He was just tilting my head back for what I was sure was going to be a serious, major snogging, when the back door slammed and Ruaraidh came into the kitchen. He stood at the door holding his wellies, looking at me standing there with my face in Devon's hands as he sat on the table in perfect kissing position. "Sorry."

"No problem," Devon said, ultracool.

Ruaraidh said good-night and walked through the kitchen. Devon waited until the kitchen door closed behind him, then lowered his head and kissed the dickens out of me. Oh, Dru, it was so . . . *fabulous*! He wasn't a wet kisser like Aidan, and his lips did interesting things on mine, and then his tongue kind of slid in and touched mine, and hoobah! I thought I was going to burst into flame right then and there. Fortunately, I didn't, and Devon kissed me a couple more times, then turned me around, swatted me on the butt, and told me to go to bed before I got into trouble. I think he was talking about sex! *fans self*

Have to go and do the lunch thing. Aunt Tim is still sicker than a dog, and since today is our last day here (Alec said we were so good, he's letting us go home early!), I'm going to make lunch for everyone. Alec made such a big deal about the horrible haggis, I thought I'd make him a gen-you-wine American lunch . . . McDonald's, yay! Fingers crossed I don't hit anything getting the Micky-D's!

Hugs and kisses,
~Em

Subject: HOTW #3
From: Mrs.Legolas@kiltnet.com
To: Dru@seattlegrrl.com
Date: 26 January 2004 2:40pm

Dru wrote:
> as if that wasn't bad enough (and I mean, really! You can
> hardly see the dent! And that's what car insurance is for,
> isn't it?), Carly said I had to pay her back for the repairs,
> and that's going to cost thousands! *Thousands!!!* How
> am I supposed to pay back thousands? She's also po'd
> about the warning I got from Miss Scott that I was going
> to get kicked off the swim team if my grades didn't get
> better. Honestly, I think my mother is just insane. Only
> half an hour of cell phone time, no Internet, no IM, no

> malling after school until my grades go up, no *anything*!
> I might as well be dead! And I have to pay back millions
> of dollars!

When did you start calling your mom by her first name? It's v. hip and all; I just wondered. And I guess I shouldn't have been crossing my fingers that I didn't hit anything (I didn't; go, me!), but should have been crossing them for you. Um . . . how did you hit a whole garage? I mean, isn't it kind of big? Wouldn't you see it and all?

Can't stay to chat—am in the middle of packing—but I wanted to send this. I'm glad you're all right and you weren't abducted by aliens or anything (hey, it could happen!), and sorry about the megagrounding. Maybe your mom will lighten up after a bit. I know Brother always goes off the deep end about stuff right away; then he relaxes after he gets used to whatever it is that sent him off in the first place. Except that time I accidentally blew up the basement. He still makes snarky comments about *that*.

Emily's Hottie of the Week
Hottie #3—Colin Farrell

- Name: Colin James Farrell
- Birthdate: March 31, 1976
- Height: 5'11"
- Famous for: movie *Tigerland*, and two seasons on *Ballykissangel* (which were fabu!). Was also nummy in *Minority Report*, *Phone Booth*, *S.W.A.T.*, and *Daredevil*.
- Skateboarding skill: unknown, so if you know, tell EHOTW
- Can he shoot a bow and arrow: doubtful

- Does he look good in tights: makes my heart wild!
- Does he look good in a blond wig: is dark haired, but would look good blond
- Coolness rating: seven out of ten pointy ears (minus three ears for—according to *Vanity Fair*—being voted Most Profane Mouth)
- Surf or motorcycle: motorcycle
- Chest test: $18
- Dream date: tour of Dublin, dinner at a pub, romantic walk in castle
- Boxers or briefs: those long-legged briefs that look sooooo sexy
- Orli rating: 87

Gotta go! Hope you're not so grounded you can't go out to see the Donnas with Timothy.

Hugs and kisses,
~Em

Subject: Back in the land of the English
From: whosyourdaddy@btinternet.co.uk
To: Dru@seattlegrrl.com
Date: 27 January 2004 10:49pm

Dru wrote:
> she said I could go to The Donnas, since I'd already bought
> the ticket, but I couldn't buy tickets to the Wrestlemania
> that's coming to Seattle, which sucks big-time! You know
> how much I love Wrestlemania! I'll die if I don't get to
> see it!

Yes, I do know how much you love that wrestling stuff, and I have to say that it's all just too, too weird of you. I mean, all those pervy guys rolling around in tights and stuff? Oh, well, I'll leave your wrestling guys alone if you stop telling me I'm crazy for being gaga over guys in kilts.

So, as you can tell, I'm back home. Note new addy (and that should be *who's* your daddy, but I couldn't use the apostrophe in the name). In case you haven't figured it out, *who's your daddy* means Devon!

Yes, yes, it's all true, I'm officially a GF again! I showed Brother the ring Devon gave me when he picked us up from the train station (we rode the train down to Edinburgh, where he and Mom picked us up), and he just did a squinty-eyed thing, and said, "How many fingers does Devon have?"

"Ten, but don't say too much about Ruaraidh having eleven, cause he's Holly's BF, and you know how easily her feelings get hurt." (Holly was using the bathroom when I said that, BTW).

"Oh. Ten. That's good. No sex, though."

"Bro*ther*!" I said, rolling my eyes.

"I can do with less of that tone, missy. Where's your luggage?"

I pointed to the pile of our bags that was at the end of the platform. "There."

He looked. "Where? Next to that mountain of suitcases?"

"It's not a mountain; it's our stuff. All of our clothes and our mementos and souvenirs and stuff."

He goggled at the bags (*mountain*, ha! It wasn't a mountain; it was just a small hill). "All that is yours? When you went up you only had two bags apiece! What did you do, buy out every shop in Scotland?"

"It's not all our stuff; Aunt Tim gave me some whiskey for you."

Brother was in a Mood all the way home. I don't know why; it didn't cost that much to ship the less important bags home.

Anyway, Holly and I had a talk on the way to Edinburgh, and I tried to really gently feel her out about Ruaraidh.

"What are you going to do with you being in England, and him in Scotland?"

She smiled at her knitting (she's knitting him another sweater). "We'll be able to e-mail each other, and call on weekends, and he's going to try to come down to Piddlington before the lambing starts in April."

"Yeah, but long-distance relationships are kind of hard, aren't they? I mean, aren't you worried that he'll . . . uh . . . he'll . . . you know, see someone else and not tell you?"

"Oh, no, Ruaraidh would never do that," she said, her eyes opened up really wide.

I almost said that he probably would, but I didn't. She was so happy, I just couldn't bring myself to ruin her first BF for her. And besides, maybe he won't be out seeing other girls, although I can't help but wonder since he seems kind of unreliable.

Boy, this relationship stuff is confusing.

Anyway, I'm going to go to bed. I don't have to be back to school until Monday (yay!), and Devon is taking tomorrow off and we're going to London for the day! He wants to show me the Dungeon Museum; isn't that sweet? It'll be our first official BF/GF date, so I'm really excited.

I've got a hottie BF, a pretty ring, and I'm away from the stinky sheep. Life is *über*-wonderful, isn't it?

Big, smoochy kisses and lots and lots of hugs,

~Em

Didn't want this book to end?

There's more waiting at **www.smoochya.com**:

Win FREE books and makeup!
Read excerpts from other books!
Chat with the authors!
Horoscopes!
Quizzes!